CALLE 10

mercury house

A
NOVEL
BY

san francisco

DANNY ROMERO

Published in the United States of America by Mercury House,
San Francisco, California, a nonprofit publishing company
devoted to the free exchange of ideas and guided by a dedica-
tion to literary values.

United States Constitution, First Amendment: Congress shall
make no law respecting an establishment of religion, or pro-
hibiting the free exercise thereof; or abridging the freedom of
speech, or of the press; or the right of the people peaceably to
assemble, and to petition the Government for a redress of
grievances.

This is a work of fiction. Any resemblence to actual locales,
events, or persons, living or dead, is coincidental.

Printed on recycled, acid-free paper and manufactured in the
United States of America.

Designed and typeset by Thomas Christensen.

Library of Congress Cataloguing-in-Publication Data:
Romero, Danny.
    Calle 10 : a novel / by Danny Romero. — 1st ed.
      p.   cm.
    ISBN 1-56279-090-0 (alk. paper)
    1. Mexican Americans—Fiction. 2. City and town life—
United States—Fiction. 3. Young men—United States—
Fiction. I. Title.
PS3568.0562C35   1996
813'.54—DC20   96-24414
                    CIP

9   8   7   6   5   4   3   2   1
FIRST EDITION

PART I

En El Norte line 72 never stopped running from Oakland, to Ciudad Jimenez, and back again. Zero boarded at 24th Street just outside of downtown. It was 1:30 AM on Saturday, and the moon was still full. El Club Paraiso had closed early because of a shooting. Zero, luckily, sneaked out of the building before the investigators arrived and was not held up for questioning.

The bus was crowded. Zero found a seat to himself near the middle of the vehicle. He sat on the aisle side. A giant black man sat across from him, sticking half out into the aisle he was so large. It looked to Zero like it would have been uncomfortable for the man to sit in the seat properly.

The giant turned toward his friend sitting behind Zero. "If it ain't rough, it ain't me," he said.

"Man, this fuckin' bus smells," said the friend behind Zero.

Zero could smell wine on the both of them and wondered if it had been a snide remark about him.

A needle-thin junkie sat four rows in front of Zero. He turned and fidgeted in his seat, scratching and jumping in his junkie agitation. He turned his pimply, brown face to the rear of the bus. It sounded to Zero like a bunch of black teenage girls sat back there, shouting and carrying on, but he did not turn around to see for himself.

"Man, the sheriff still be following us," said the friend behind Zero.

"They can follow all they motherfuckin' want," said the giant half in the aisle, "but they can't cross no motherfuckin' county line.... If it ain't rough, it ain't me. I'm telling you...." He danced in his seat to a rhythm only he could hear. A scar ran down the left side of his face. A thick and knobby one, it started above his eye and continued down past his cheek. "It's that motherfuckin' bitch that's driving the bus got those motherfuckin' sheriffs following us," said the giant. He danced some more in his seat.

The female driver of the bus pulled to the curb to pick up more passengers. A heavyset and haggard-looking black man seated near the driver shouted, "Don't fall asleep back there soldier." He wore a green army jacket and a blue watch cap. His beard and moustache were overgrown. "You know what happened last time you fell asleep," he went on. Giggles came from the rear of the bus. He talked about marines and lectured how they needed to make it out of Vietnam.

"Man, don't be shouting at me, drunk motherfucker," said the giant with the scar.

"You know I ain't talking to you," said the marine. "Don't you start with me."

"No, you don't start with me," said the giant.

A young black student boarded the bus. He was dressed in gray slacks and a black turtleneck sweater. He seated himself up front and carried a briefcase with gold lettering spelling out OAKLAND JUNIOR COLLEGE. He wore headphones and dark glasses.

"Wake up back there soldier!" shouted the marine again.

Another black man ran past Zero up the aisle and sat behind the driver. He wore eye makeup and moved and sounded like a woman. His pants were falling off, and more than half of his white briefs showed. "Lady, puh-leeze don't call the po-lease on these crazy fools," he said.

"If it ain't rough, it ain't me," shouted the giant.

The one behind the driver turned, his hands pressed together in prayer. "Puh-leeze quiet down or the driver gon' call the po-lease. Put us all off the goddamn bus."

"Hey, fuck the po-lease," said the giant.

"Wake up soldier back there," said the marine. "I don't wanna catch you dozing off again."

"Oh puh-leeze be quiet."

"Shut up, you dumb sissy," said the giant. He turned to his friend. "We get off at the transit station and walk down to Calle 4. I can get some there from homeboy."

"Oh puh-leeze be quiet," said the sissy. He sat behind the driver with his pants half off. "The woman's gon' call the po-lease." He grew more disturbed, making pleading faces to all on the bus. His friends in the rear cried, their queer laughter screeching, "Pppuuuhhh-llleeeeeezzzeee you dumb niggas gon' get us all thrown off the bus."

The one with headphones and turtleneck sweater stood abruptly. He slammed the window next to him shut, then slammed shut those around him also, standing and moving quickly about the bus from window to window. He sat back down.

"Mmmaaannn, FUCK YOU," said the giant. He and

his friend stood and opened all the windows on the bus. A cold wind blew through it. "What the fuck you think this is, motherfucker," said the giant.

Up front the sissy sat wide-eyed with fear, staring at those that were quarreling. "Oh puh-leeze don't start nothing," said the sissy.

The turtleneck looked up and said, "Say, brother, what's going on?"

"I ain't your brother, motherfucker," said the giant. "This ain't your bus."

"It's cold in here, brother," said the dark glasses.

"FUCK YOU," said the giant. "I said I ain't your brother."

The junkie up front turned his sweaty face toward the scene.

The giant's friend said, "Man, we want fresh air."

"We can take it outside," said the giant.

"Wake up back there. I'm not gonna tell you again," yelled the marine.

Again the bus pulled over to the curb. The sheriff's car now stopped in front of it. The lights turned and flashed through the front windshield of the bus.

Zero never thought he would live en Ciudad Jimenez. He used to think he had more sense, then came to realize there were quite a few things in his thirty years of life that he never thought he would do and had already done, and that were themselves, some of them especially, against any notion of sense or intelligence he may have claimed to possess.

He knew the manager of the rooming house, Henry, from

work. Henry worked on the first floor in the print shop. He ran a small ABdick offset printer, making labels, business cards, letterhead, and envelopes for the university. Zero worked answering the telephones, typing up letters, and filing. They drank and smoked grass together on the roof. Zero once went to a party at Henry's, back when his old lady and kids still lived with him in Oakland, and stayed the entire weekend.

When he decided to rent a room from Henry, he had no place else to go. His girlfriend, La Wilma, said he could not stay with her. The apartment was too small, she said, and he still too much of a jerk at times. He could not afford to live alone, not sure either that it would not drive him crazy altogether. Clear the fuck out of my stinking mind, Zero liked to say.

The bus did not take him all the way home at this time of the night. To get there he would have to walk along a darkened underpass below the tracks from the transit station trains. The bus parked at Calle 19 and the Boulevard.

Zero waited at the back door, but the driver would not open it. He went to the front, letting the crew of young black sissies go first. Some wore cut-off jeans and had breast implants; one wore a blonde wig. Zero stayed a few feet behind them as they giggled and pinched each other off the bus.

A lanky Asian man now sat near the bus driver. "Hey, how you doing?" he said to Zero.

Zero did not recognize the man and was puzzled by the greeting. "Yeah, all right," said Zero, stepping off the bus. There was always the chance that Zero had met the man while he was drunk and was now unable to remember it. It was a common enough occurrence. Zero would be with La Wilma riding the bus through the worst part of the city, and some old wino, prostitute, junkie, or gangster would come up to him and begin where some conversation had left off some time in the past when Zero was in a blackout. La Wilma would say, "Who was that, ese?"

Zero was never able to say for certain who the person was or why they seemed to know more than just his name. And La Wilma would point this out to make him feel foolish, and he would. The bitch, he would think, as he hurried her away.

The Asian man may have been the crazy Thai guy, he figured, as he walked down the Boulevard. The crazy Thai guy lived near him while Zero was studying at the university.

It was late, and el taco truck was missing from the parking lot of the Jalisco Bar. Zero thought el taco truck had the best food in all of El Norte. It reminded him of his childhood en El Sur, growing up en la Ciudad de las Calles. Zero felt privileged to live near el taco truck and ate there several times a week. On special days he ate there twice, days when he was feeling lucky, important, or rich; though he knew in reality he was none of those things. Only on downers did he feel like a slick hipster these days.

Within seconds everyone from the bus scattered off into the darkness of Ciudad Jimenez. Zero walked at a brisk pace through the darkened underpass. He glanced at shadows moving up above along the dirt embankment leading to the tracks.

When he arrived home, Henry was still awake. He was

standing on the front porch when Zero walked up. Henry stood in only boxer shorts, worn thin and almost transparent, drinking a sixteen-ounce can of malt liquor. His long hair was tangled and uncombed.

"Say, bro', my casa es tu casa," said Henry, swaying on his feet. "You know what I'm saying, bro'? My casa es tu casa." Henry shook his head back into focus. His face was bloated and his complexion blotchy from alcohol. He had sinus trouble from a twice-broken nose. "Hey, bro', how 'bout a hamburger? I was just gonna cook some up." He staggered on into the house, walking first into the doorframe, then stopping and turning around. "Eh, I cleaned up all that shit out of the hallway like I said I was gonna, bro'." He then continued into the house, through la entrada, bouncing from one wall to the other down the dark hallway. Zero followed and stood in the doorway of the kitchen.

"See, bro', I have to cook up this burger," said Henry. He stood at a counter in the middle of the room in his underwear. He had a handful of raw hamburger squeezed between his fingers and oozing out from his clenched fist. On the counter was a larger mound of raw meat. Near Henry stood two plastic garbage bags, three-feet tall each, one filled with trash, the other with aluminum cans. Flies buzzed back and forth between the bags and the mound of meat. The walls of the room were stained with grease. "I defrosted it earlier and have to cook it up," said Henry. He absentmindedly moved the handful of hamburger up to his mouth and burped into it.

"That bitch was supposed to let me have the kids," said

Henry, "but we had a fight when I went down to pick them up. That bitch." He burped into his hand again, then took a drink from the can of malt liquor in the other one. "So how 'bout a hamburger?" he asked.

"Nah, man," said Zero. "Not right now."

Henry looked like he was offended. "Yeah, all right, bro'. Whatever. Hey, don't think you offended me, even if you did," said Henry. "I mean, when a man asks another man to share a meal with him, and since you are staying in this house till you and your old lady can work it out.... Hey, bro', I admire that. But I ain't offended. Don't worry 'bout it."

Zero was exasperated. "Eh, I don't wanna eat what you been burping on all night," he said.

Henry stood at the counter flattening out patties of hamburger between the palms of his hands. Every other minute he would daintily pick up the can with greasy fingers and drink. His body was pale. His chest was sunken. The days of a daily jailhouse regimen of one hundred push-ups and sit-ups were long gone. "You say something, bro'?" asked Henry, looking up at Zero in the doorway. "You wanna hamburger?" Henry stepped over to the sink, raised his can of malt liquor and poured some down his throat. He put the empty into the sink with a pile of dirty dishes.

On the stove a griddle lay on the flame. Bent out of shape and no longer flat, it wobbled on the fire at a crooked angle. The plastic handle was missing, and now there was only a metal rod to hold onto. Hot grease from the meat pooled within the griddle's half-inch depth. Henry grabbed the metal rod with his bare hand. "Hhheeeyyy ssshhhiiittt!" he screamed. He reached for a pot holder from a hook on the wall above the stove.

"You should turn down the fire," said Zero.

Henry ignored him. The flames grew larger, moving up the sides of the griddle. "You wanna beer, bro'?" asked Henry. He put the pot holder on the stove top and turned around, reaching into the refrigerator and bringing out two cans.

"Nah, that's all right," said Zero. He stepped over to the stove and turned down the flame.

"You're still on the wagon?" asked Henry, surprised. He popped a can open, keeping the other near by. "No sense in putting this back inside," he said. "How long you been dry now?" Henry tilted his head back and ceremoniously drained half the can.

"It's been one hundred days since they carried me off kicking and screaming to the hospital," said Zero. His left ear was still ringing from the last drunk.

"Yeah, all right, bro'," said Henry, uninterested and hoping Zero did not go on. He did not want to hear how Zero's life was changed by AA. "I already know all that crap about AA, ese," said Henry. "All about it, homeboy, pero, yo soy mas loco. This is it, ese. Mi vida loca!" He leaned his head back and howled, "Oooooowwww!"

"You wanna hamburger, bro'?" asked Henry. "I have to cook it up because I defrosted it today. And I don't want it to spoil." He turned a patty over, sizzling.

"Are you gonna eat one?" asked Zero. He watched Henry

carelessly flipping the mounds of hamburger with a too-small spatula. Grease popped all over the stove. Flames grew larger, splashing and crackling.

"Hey, I think you're gonna have a real problem if the grease drips into the fire," said Zero, pointing to the stove.

"Eh, it'll be all right, bro'," said Henry. "It'll be all right." He took another drink. "Hey, you know, I bet that video show is on the television right now, ese. You know which one I'm talkin' 'bout, bro'? What do they call it?" Henry grabbed his drink and ran past Zero out of the kitchen, down the hallway and into the sala.

Zero waited in the kitchen. The music grew louder coming from the sala. Henry howled to the music. Zero could hear him stumbling around the room, trying to dance. "Hhheeeyyy Zzzeeerrrooo come check this out. Oooooowww...." screamed Henry. A lamp and table fell over.

Zero cooked until past dawn. Henry slept on the floor of the sala.

When Henry next saw him, Zero sat at the table with his friend Ray. They were smoking marijuana resin they had scraped out of Zero's pipe. The smoke was harsh, but powerful.

Ray said, "Man, I should have let you buy me that other can of beer." He drank the last of the can of Miller High Life. "Damn you, carnal, that tastes good," he said. He smacked his lips. Then Henry walked in from the entrada, carrying twelve tall cans of malt liquor.

Henry said to Zero, "Eh, what happened to that hamburger I had in the freezer? Do you know, bro'? You should let me know if you're gonna use my food. I might have been saving that for when the next time the kids come over for the weekend, and we might want to barbecue or something. You know what I'm saying, bro'?"

"Eh, I don't know what happened to your hamburger," said Zero. And later, as they were wont to do, they all three sat around and talked about Chicanos and which one of them was the better one.

Henry still wore an ink-covered apron from work. He stood up. "Man," he said, rocking on his feet, "Yo soy El Nose mas loco de Calle 19. Rifamos, ese. Puro Chicano y puro loco." And in his mind he stood seventeen years earlier en la esquina de Calle 19 and the Boulevard with a bloody bumper jack in his hand, and a homeboy gunned down near his Chevy. "You know, ese," he said, "Chicano!" He stood up straighter and held his head high, thrusting his chest forward. "Puro Chicano y puro loco," he said. He took a too-large drink from his malt liquor and gagged on it, doubling over. He sat back down, coughing.

Zero spoke up, "Hey, I went to college. For eight years to get my BA." Henry and Ray ignored Zero's comments. "It took me so long," he went on, "because I had to work to pay for booze and rent."

Henry stood back up again. "We're talkin' 'bout Chicano, ese," he said. "You went to the gabacho government school."

Zero ignored Henry. They all three sat silent, smoking and drinking. On one wall hung a color television from the ceiling. The opposite wall was covered with children's drawings and fingerpaintings. There were pictures of ghosts and goblins, lowriders, Chicano power clenched brown fists, crucifixes and pachucos. The window facing the street was always boarded up. Nearby there was a mirror on the wall. A doorway led into the kitchen; another led down a hallway to a shower and toilet. There were bedrooms along one side of the house and upstairs.

A smaller table held the telephone and a few books and magazines. Above it was a cabinet with glass doors. It was mostly filled with empty beer cans, match books, shot glasses, zig-zag rolling papers, tequila bottles, ashtrays, and crumpled paper. Henry broke the silence of the resin smoke.

"I used to have a '55 Bel-Air with a pearl paint job, Cragar mags all around, chrome all over and hydraulics. It was chingon, ese," he said.

Ray put his empty can into a trash bag filled with them in the corner of the room. He grabbed another one from on top of the table. "Eh, I don't work no more," he said, "thanks to Workers Compensation. Thank you. Thank you. I worked hard for the money, for that money. They told me if they ever find out I'm faking they will throw me in prison. She told me this. This bitch I have to see about my case from time to time. And I do mean bitch." He opened the can of malt liquor.

"Sounds good to me," said Zero. "Not working."

"Eh, and fuck the gabacho government," Ray went on. "That's Chicano. Los gabachos government been cheating us from the beginning. They ripped us off our land.... Hey, I don't care 'bout no treaty of Guadalupe or whatever it was. That land was taken with a gun, and that's how we take it back.... I wasn't around back then in 1841 or whenever they had that shit, so I don't have to accept nothing. Sabes que, ese? No treaty. No shit. This is Aztlan. Puro Chicano. Fuck the acceptance. Assimilation. Fuck that shit, homeboy. I'm forty years old, and I get more Chicano everyday. Sabes que?" Ray stood and leaned against the wall with the drawings. He was oval shaped. Over his shoulders were a sombrero on one side and an Uzi on the other. He leaned back all droopy from the booze and slant-eyed from the resin. He looked up and said, "You know, ese, I am lowriding right now."

Henry stood and clapped, cheering, "Orale. Orale. Chicano Power." He danced drunkenly in the crowded space, singing, "Vamos a bailar, Chicano.... Vamos a chingar, Chicano...."

Zero said, "I used to cruise Whittier Boulevard in East Los Angeles when I was a kid. Boyle Heights. Before they closed it down and moved it to Montebello, now Pico Rivera. You know the song by Thee Midniters?" He shouted, "Let's take a trip down Whittier Boulevard. Beep. Beep. Arriba. Arriba." He smiled, remembering that song was the opening theme to the Huggy Boy Show, the one and only Chicano television show. It was an afternoon teenage dance program carried on a UHF station. Zero used to watch it after school when he was eleven years old. It was short-lived, canceled because of gang violence on the set. "Like in the movies," he went on, "with the cars going up and down.... Believe it. Or don't." He pulled at his nose.

"Yeah. I been down there, too," said Henry, reluctantly. "It was live, I have to admit."

Ray butted in, "Eh, I make my old lady cook beans all the time. We always got a pot over at my house."

"Yeah, I can tell from the smell at your house," said Henry, "that you always got some bean eating going on."

"Yeah, shit," said Ray, "like this place is the Taj Mahal."

Henry filled the pipe with resin. He winked at Zero. "Eh, Zero," he said, "it sounds like Ray don't like the place where we call home."

"No," said Ray, "that's not what I meant. You're always trying to start trouble, man, Henry."

"Okay, I'm just kidding, bro', you know it," said Henry. He held his hand out to shake. "All right?" asked Henry. Ray slapped the palm of it as hard as he could.

Henry pushed his chair back and stood. He hiked up his pants. "You will find around here, Zero, sometimes," he said, "that there are these pesky little moscos, buzzing around here at odd times of the day and night." He pulled his hand back as if stung by a bee. "Oh," he said, "and I think one just bit me right now."

Ray and Zero were laughing. Ray said, "Eh, are you sure it wasn't on your ass?"

Henry changed to a more serious tone in his voice. "You ready?" he asked Ray.

Ray stood, pulling up his pants. "Eh, I'm ready, " he said. He poured some malt liquor down his throat, then held the palm of his left hand out in front of him.

"Keep it steady," said Henry, winding his arm with a windmill motion. "I wanna get a good shot at it." His hand came crashing down on Ray's palm. Back and forth they went.

"Eh, that didn't hurt."

"Fuck you."

"Fuck me?"

"Ha, ha, ha."

"Fuck you."

Henry said, "Man, that didn't even hurt. And you used your wedding ring, bro'. I see how you are." He stopped to take a drink. "You see, but I don't got no wedding ring. I took it off in the courtroom and threw it at that bitch. Fuck her! Sabes que? You know what I'm saying, bro'?" He nodded over to Zero. To Ray he said, "Stop flinching. No flinching…. Hey are you gonna keep that hand still, or what?"

Ray held his hand out, then pulled it back before Henry could hit it. "Okay. Okay," he said, putting his hand out and pulling it back before Henry could hit it.

Zero sat there watching, laughing, and smoking the pipe full of resin. He passed it to Ray.

Henry said, "Hey, none of that stalling. Hey, I see you. Stalling time is what you are doing. Give me that." Henry removed the pipe from Ray's mouth. "Stalling time is what you were doing," he said, smoking the resin.

Ray said, "As a Chicano I am always only an arm's length from the jailhouse. The gabacho government wants to arrest me for walking down the street. Or for my Pancho Villa moustache...."

"Cabron," said Henry. "I thought you was gonna take off that ring there, bro'. Don't be a sissy about it. This is man to man. Mano a mano. But if you need to use that ring ... go right ahead, bro'. I can take it.... I thought we were all men here, but ..."

"Man, fuck you," said Ray, "I'm taking it off. Don't worry 'bout it. I don't need it. Here you go." Ray removed the gold band and placed it on the table. He then braced himself for the slap from Henry. "Come on, cabron," he said, "let me feel your little mosco." He held out his scarlet palm, then pulled it back and danced around the room. "Man," he said, "when you gonna get some music in this place. At my house it's always on full blast. My wife and kids they complain." He sang, "I am el cabron fat loco. Si, yo soy. El gordito locito. Cabron."

"Come on. Come on," said Henry.

"Let me drink my drink, cabron," said Ray. He stopped dancing and drank.

"All right. All right," said Henry, sounding reasonable. "You don't have to get upset. You don't have to scream for some." He acted like he was going to unzip his trousers. "Here you go, bro'," he said. "All you want, but please watch it with the teeth this time. Okay?"

Ray danced around the room again. "Eh, fuck you," he said. "Don't bother taking it out. We wouldn't be able to find it." He laughed at his own joke loudly, danced, and waved to Zero.

"You found it last time all right, bro'," said Henry.

"Eh, fuck you," said Ray. "I'm the better Chicano because every year I go to the Cinco de Mayo concert, and I get so fucked up I can't remember a thing." He screamed, "Oooooowww!"

Henry looked offended. "Ahem," he said, clearing his throat. "Are you saying you don't remember *this?*" He pointed to his crotch and made a face of disappointment. "You hurt me when you say you don't remember," he said.

"Man, fuck you," said Ray, spinning around. "You know sometimes, Henry, you are seriously unfunny."

Henry made a baby face at Ray.

"When I was twelve," said Zero, "we used to sniff paint in Francisco Vasquez's garage. Man, you know, only the best. Five star gold and silver. Metallica. The good stuff. Then we'd go and write on walls. Sniff and write. Sniff and write. A couple of years later we were smoking Angel Dust."

Ray signaled to Zero, putting a fore and middle finger together in the shape of a V, and pressing it to his lips. Henry had his back turned. He switched on the television, moving through the channels. "Hey, bro', what channel's that video show on?" asked Henry.

Zero said, "Hey, Ray, let's have a cigarette."

"Orale, cabron," said Ray. He smiled his big white teeth.

"Let's go. Let's go." He turned to Henry and said, "Hey, I'm gonna take a break, motherfucker."

Henry bugged his eyes out in mock astonishment. He then began with a phony British accent, acting all prim and proper, "You gonna tell me now, bro', that you're gonna quit this now. Ahem.... Well.... Yes.... If you must quit, well then quit. If you cannot take it, then I say quit while you are still alive." He stroked his chin.

"Fuck you, cabron," said Ray, excited. "I'm not quitting." He took a quick drink, some of it dribbling down the front of his shirt. He smiled in embarrassment and hurried outside. "I'll be right back, motherfucker," he said.

Henry sat down at the table, looking up at the television. "I'll be here waiting," he said, waving Ray along.

Zero followed Ray. Outside they both stood on the steps of the house. "Can I have a cigarette?" asked Zero.

Ray was caught off guard. "Oh, you don't have none," he said. He held his left hand in the air. It looked like a lobster claw, burning red and not-human. "I thought you wanted to come out here and have a smoke?"

"I do, but I don't have anymore cigarettes," said Zero. "Can I have one?"

"Sure, bro'," said Ray, hesitantly. "I think I might have enough, an extra one." He brought out a new pack from his pocket, working with only one hand, and tapping it against his thigh. "Good thing I'm right-handed, huh, bro'?" said Ray. He tore the cellophane wrapper off with his teeth, then took one out. He put the box back in his pocket.

"Eh, can I have a cigarette?" asked Zero.

"Oh yeah, bro'. I forgot," said Ray. He struggled to take another cigarette out.

"Let me have two," said Zero. "So I don't have to ask you again." They passed matches between themselves.

"Henry gets fucking crazy when he drinks," said Ray. He sucked on his can of malt liquor, then the cigarette. "I mean fucking crazy when he gets drunk." He sucked on the can of malt liquor. "Cabron," he said, "look at my hand. I hope it's not broken." He held out the red swollen blob. "Henry gets fucking crazy when he drinks," said Ray. He sucked on his cigarette.

Zero was not listening. Here I am, he thought, thirty years old, college educated, working as a clerk in a print shop and renting a room en Ciudad Jimenez. La Wilma kept mocking him, telling him he lived in a halfway house. Still, Zero knew he was a long way from El Sur, y la Ciudad de las Calles. Perro callejero he was in those years, now still to a degree, but smarter, he hoped. He was not proud of that time in his life, but honest about it.

"Eh, you know what," said Ray. "It's too bad you don't drink no more. You can't have any fun. You sit there and smoke weed, but you're too quiet. You never get loud or anything like that. I don't know, bro', don't you ever feel like drinking?"

"All the time," said Zero.

"Oh yeah," said Ray, now hopeful. "Here you go, bro'. Have some of mine." He held his can out to Zero.

Zero pushed the can away. Up until now all his life had been one screeching skid out of control. "Forget it," he said.

"Come on, man," said Ray. "What's the big deal? You're too young to be an alcoholic."

"Whatever," said Zero. He lit the second cigarette.

"Hey, I'm gonna get home right now," said Ray. He stretched and yawned. "My old lady is gonna be pissed 'bout my hand. Fuck, I hope it's not broken. Fuck Henry. He gets fuckin' crazy when he drinks. I'll see you later on, bro'." Ray waddled off the porch. He held his left hand up swollen and red: with his right hand he brought the can of malt liquor up to his mouth for a drink. "Eh, I hope I can drive," he said. "See you later, bro'."

"Later on," said Zero. He watched Ray walk away from the house. Ray threw the empty can on the lawn and went across the street to his car. He stuck his good hand down the front of his pants, straightening out his dick and balls. He then got in his car and drove off, one misshapen hand sticking out the car window as he drove.

The next day after work Henry gave Zero a ride on his motorcycle over to La Wilma's. It was just before nine at night, and the temperature was seventy-five degrees. They both wished they had not brought a jacket to work that day.

Earlier in the day Henry had asked Zero if he could go over to the liquor store for him and bring him back a couple of tall cans of malt liquor. "You know how it is, bro'," Henry said to Zero.

"Is two going to be enough?" asked Zero.

"Yeah, that's all I need," said Henry. "Just to make me feel a little better. I'm gonna be cool for a couple of days. You know what I mean?"

But by the end of the day Henry had done better than that. Leroy took him up to the roof for some grass. It took his mind off his troubles. And the two cans of malt liquor worked so well he sneaked out of the building with his press still running and bought himself a third can. His head was on straight after that.

"How far we going, bro'?" asked Henry. He towered over the motorcycle, the handlebars in his hands. It was a small .175-horsepower Honda. Henry had taken over the payments from his nephew. He liked to brag that it did not take him long to pay off the debt.

"Down by where Tyrone used to live," said Zero. "You know where that is?"

Henry put on his helmet. "Yeah, I know," he said, his voice now garbled. "You seen that motherfucker Tyrone lately? He owes some rent."

"Not lately," said Zero. He stepped over the back of the bike and sat down. He pushed the foot pegs down and rested his feet on top of them.

Henry held the bike up. "You ready, bro'?" he asked. He started the engine and they pulled out of the parking lot. Henry used the bike whenever he could because of the money he saved on gasoline. For five dollars he could ride for the entire week, but with his car for only two days if he was lucky, which he never was.

The pair pulled into traffic, heading south on Christian

Avenue. There are a lot of people out on the street tonight, thought Zero. His knuckles were white, gripping the small bar on the back of the seat. Henry sped up too quickly, catching Zero off guard. His feet came up off the foot pegs for an instant, the lower part of his body airborne. He came back down on the seat, his hands still gripping the bar at the back of it.

He found it difficult to breath when he faced straight on into the oncoming wind. He turned his face to the left and his shoulder down into the wind. Henry passed over some railroad tracks at too fast a speed for Zero, and once again he was airborne. This time he let his hands go, flying out over his head; his feet came up, legs splayed outward. He came back down on the seat and grabbed the bar behind the seat. Henry did not slow down.

Zero stood in the entrance of the building. La Wilma lived three flights up and in the rear. He pressed the buzzer for apartment number eleven. There was no answer. He stepped over to the heavy wooden door. On either side of it were windows. He looked into the window on the right and saw a couch and table in the lobby, and stairs leading to the upper floors, but no one to let him in.

He walked around the corner of the building, through an alleyway to the courtyard, and looked up at her apartment. He saw a light on in the kitchen. He walked back over to the front door and leaned on the buzzer some more.

La Wilma's voice came over the intercom. "Who is it?" she asked, sounding cheerful.

"It's me, Zero," he said. He thought, who the fuck else would be coming over at this time?

There was silence.

Zero pressed the buzzer again. Still there was no answer. He leaned on it a little heavier.

"Quit buzzing the fuckin' buzzer, ese," said La Wilma over the intercom. "Go away."

Zero said, "What do you mean, 'go away'?! I just got here."

"It's too late," said La Wilma. "Go home, Zero."

Zero pressed the buzzer once again.

"Get the fuck away, ese," said La Wilma.

"Come on now, let me up," said Zero, feeling like a fool already. He knew she could not hear him unless she pressed the listen button in her apartment while he spoke. If she did not, he would only talk to the wall. He leaned on the buzzer.

"Quit the fuckin' buzzer, Zero. Go away."

Zero pressed it again.

"Bastard. Get the fuck away from here, ese."

Zero looked over his shoulder. An elderly Asian man and woman stood at the door, searching for their keys. Man and wife, thought Zero. "How you doing?" he said to them, feeling stupid. He pressed the buzzer again to contact La Wilma.

"Bastard. Get the fuck away from here, ese."

"I want to tell you something," said Zero.

"What do you want, bastard," said La Wilma. The Asian couple still stood there, listening.

"I want to tell you something," said Zero. He smiled at the couple, trying to make light of his situation.

"Tell me from there."

Zero said, "Eh, I don't want to tell everyone in the street." He watched the couple proceed into the building. The door slowly moved toward closing. "I want to tell you in person," he said. Zero looked in the window and saw the couple begin up the stairs. He slipped into the building just before the door closed.

He waited a few minutes before climbing the stairs. Near the third floor he ran into two young women walking down. They both were drinking beers though neither of them looked old enough to do so legally. They carried baskets of laundry and crowded onto the stairs above Zero. One was blonde. The other a brunette. They both wore short-shorts, and bare breasts wiggled underneath loose t-shirts. "Hey, how you doing," said the brunette as they squeezed by each other. Zero just smiled and nodded his head. College kids, he thought, maneuvering himself between the two of them. He felt the blonde's firm, still-springy ass brush against his crotch. He was not sure if it was by accident or not.

At the top of the stairs he turned and watched them continue on down. The bottoms of their asses—Zero's favorite part where ass meets legs, creating a space to grab hold of—peeked out from the bottoms of their shorts, pale in contrast to their long tanned legs.

On the third floor Zero rang the bell to apartment number eleven. He stepped to the side a bit. La Wilma, he knew, would look through the peephole before opening the door. He did not want her to see him before she opened the door.

The door opened. La Wilma kept the chain on. It hung across her face. She was naked underneath her bathrobe, and her hair was still wet. "How'd you get in the building, you bastard," said La Wilma.

"These people let me in downstairs," said Zero.

"Go home, Zero," said La Wilma. "I don't feel like talking to you." She started to close the door.

Zero stuck his hand in the doorway. "Hey, wait," he said. "What's going on? What the fuck did I do?"

La Wilma kept the door open. "What's the idea of coming by so late, ese? What kinda excuse you got this time? And I better not find out you been talkin' to that bitch," she said.

Zero stood at the door, looking in through the few inches of space. He saw a fat nipple within his grasp. "What's the big deal?" he asked, reaching for it.

La Wilma did not think it was funny. She struck at his fingers with a torque wrench she kept behind the door, missing. It hit the wood with a dull thud, gouging the wall.

"What's the big deal?" said La Wilma. "What time'd you get out of work, cabron? I'm sure you been workin' all this time. I bet, ese. You just hang around with your stupid friends smoking weed and when you get tired of them you come over here, thinking you can get some pussy. That's what the big deal is, ese."

Zero stuck his foot in the door. "Hey, I had to work late," he lied. "Then I waited for Henry so I can give him the money for rent, but I have to wait so he gets off work and drives me over to the bank, then here. You know how slow he does things?" La Wilma was no longer pushing the door from the other side.

"Don't lie to me," she said. She pushed the door on his foot. "You think I'm stupid, or what, ese?"

Zero said, "If I knew you were in such a bad mood, I wouldn't have come over."

"Fuck you and your bad mood, ese," said La Wilma, pushing on the door now harder. "I was fine until you came over … you fuckin' liar. If you would've called you would've known I didn't want your ass over."

"Eh, I did try to call," lied Zero. "But I couldn't get through." The pushing on the other side stopped. He put his hand around the door, his fingers inside the apartment.

"You fuckin' liar," said La Wilma. She pushed the door with all her weight. "I haven't been on the phone all fuckin' day."

Zero's foot in the door saved his hand from being crushed. He went on, "Eh, I don't know. I didn't say it was busy. I just couldn't get a connection. Eh, I don't know, maybe the phone at work is fucked up." He waited a minute for an answer. There was none. With his fingers he flashed a peace sign inside the apartment and held it there for another minute. He then reached for the chain and tried to remove it.

La Wilma threw her weight against the door, wedging his foot in the doorway. She grabbed the torque wrench and drove the handle down onto the top of his foot in a stabbing motion. With one shoulder against the door, she brought the wrench handle down over and over again, harder and harder onto the top of his foot.

Zero screamed and struggled to dislodge himself from the doorway. "Man, you're fuckin' stupid," he said. His foot came loose, and he limped in a circle in front of the door. "I don't know what the fuck your problem is," he said. "You know that?"

The door was still open, held by the chain. He limped over to it quietly. He stood outside it, trying his best not to make any noise. He peered inside and saw the torque wrench leaning against the wall within reach. He slipped his arm in quickly and grabbed it, bringing it outside the apartment. He stood on his good foot, leaning his back against the wall; he hoped his foot was not broken. He slammed the wrench lightly onto the door with a thunk, smiling at the piece of wood the wrench took out of the door. He let the wrench drop to the carpet of the hallway and stuck his arm into the apartment. He flashed his fingers into a peace sign, once again. "Hey, come on now, let me in," he said. He waved his middle finger around.

La Wilma threw her weight against the door.

"Eh, shit...." said Zero.

La Wilma latched onto the fleshy part of his upper arm with her fingernails, digging them into the skin, tearing his shirt, fibers of pain unraveling.

Zero screamed; the door jerked back and forth onto and off of his arm. He stood up on his bad foot and screamed some more, pounding on the door with his other hand. "You're fuckin' out of your mind," he said, pulling on his arm. It came free, and in his effort he fell over backward. He lay on the floor for a minute, then looked up.

The brunette from the stairs stood over him. "You all right?" she asked, smiling.

Zero could feel the blood rush to his face. He hoped La Wilma was not listening or watching. He could see up the woman's t-shirt as she leaned over him and it fell away from her body: two breasts the size of grapefruits, standing away from the body, nipples turned upward, the belly not as big as the bustline.

He closed his eyes in embarrassment. "Yeah," he said, "I'm all right." He smelled one of them pass on his left side, the other on the right, both of them seeming to brush against him ever so lightly. He heard them giggle, but did not watch them jiggle down the hallway.

After they had passed and he heard a door close behind them, Zero picked himself up onto his elbows. He looked over at La Wilma's door. It was closed. Near it there was a paper bag, filled, he knew, with his belongings.

PART II

From out of Tyrone's second-floor window, looking down, Zero could see Henry and Ray standing among weeds in the backyard. The pair stood near the driveway. In it was a rusted 1977 Pontiac station wagon with a silver paint job and chrome rims. It had been there for a month now up on blocks. Behind them and along the rear fence and covering half the yard was a wooden shed, now leaning and rotting. Only Henry had a key to the padlock. He held it on a giant jailer's ring in his hand.

Zero pressed a finger against his left nostril and snorted a large intake of air to help clear the right passageway. He could taste the heroin.

Outside Ray took a botella from his windbreaker pocket. It looked like a half pint of tequila to Zero. Ray unscrewed the cap and took a short taste. He handed it to Henry. Ray lit a cigarette and puffed on it rapidly.

Zero rested his head on the windowsill, still looking out. He could feel the narcotic coursing through his insides, swelling up like an ocean inside of him and taking over. He knew the pair could not see him from where they were. The shadows grew larger behind the two of them. Henry bent toward Ray, as if whispering. He looked repeatedly over his shoulder to check to see that no one walked up on them.

Tyrone came back into the room. He was tugging at his afro with a pick, trying to work some tangle out. He was six-feet tall and lean, dressed in camouflage army fatigue pants and a yellowing t-shirt. He wore orange-tinted aviator glasses. One of the arms was fastened together with Scotch tape. He stood in the middle of the room for a moment, tugging, his face in a grimace and his arms above his head. "Man, motherfucker," he said, then crossed the room and sat down on his bed.

Zero saw the pair outside had moved over to the station wagon. Ray rested his ass against the front hood of the car, the botella on top of it. The looks on their faces were no longer friendly. Henry, every now and again, would poke his finger into Ray's chest to emphasize his point.

Tyrone said, "Those motherfuckers still out there." He tapped his finger against the side of the hypodermic needle to get rid of the trapped bubbles of air.

"Uh-huh," said Zero. He closed the curtain and turned, slowly, back toward Tyrone.

"Dab some water on the insides of your nose there, so you can get the shit out of your nosehairs," said Tyrone. He tapped the side of the needle again. "You gonna feel it," he said, "but not like you should. I can skin pop you real easy if you want. That's how I started out, but now I know there ain't no better thing than for me to take this all the way to the motherfuckin' hoop." He put the needle down for a moment and slurped some wine out of a bottle of Thunderbird. He tied a rubber hose around his arm. He pulled on one end of it with his clenched teeth, then he pumped the arm up and down, opening and closing his fist. "Hair-on. 'Caine. I'll shoot up any motherfuckin' thang." He found his spot and put the needle to the skin. "My battle motherfuckin' wound," he said, "that's what I tell everybody. And it's true. I got this motherfucker back in Vietnam." He pressed the point into the vein, then pushed half the load into his arm, drawing it back into the needle, filling it with blood and dope mixed together. He pumped it in again, then back out, then all in again in a flash. His eyes turned up to whiteness.

Zero looked outside again. The two in the yard now stood shaking hands and patting each other on the back. Henry kissed Ray on the cheek, Ray taking a swing at him because of it. They hooked their arms together like lovers, passing the botella back and forth and drinking.

"It's dripping down," said Zero. His voice sounded odd to him. Almost as if he was underwater.

Tyrone stretched out on the bed, surrounded by newspapers. He put his head against the wall behind him and brought his legs up, tearing paper. His head hung down from his neck onto his chest. Up above him hung a bayonet knife from a string attached to a hook on the wall. "This is pretty good shit," he said, "better than that motherfuckin' codiena you wanted those motherfuckin' doctors to give you. Give me the motherfuckin' hair-on.... You don't need no motherfuckin' cane." He lifted his head to say this, wiping drool from the corner of his mouth. He scratched behind his ear, then went on. "You know you just thought they be giving you some motherfuckin' narcotics and then they go and say the foot ain't even broke. But that don't mean it don't hurt like a motherfucker." He reached to the nightstand near the bed for his box of Menthols, brought the package up to his mouth, and took a cigarette out with his teeth. He held the pack out to Zero.

Zero felt more sluggish. He snorted and rubbed the side of his nose. The heroin dripped down the back of his throat. He dipped his fingertips into a glass of water near him and dabbed at his nostrils. He waved off Tyrone's offer. "Nah, that's all right," he said.

"Shit," said Tyrone, breaking into a smile of rotting teeth. "You scared to smoke in this motherfuckin' place or what?" He put the box back on the nightstand and picked up a plastic lighter. He struck the flint a couple of times before the flame came on.

Zero said, "I don't feel like it."

"I hear you," said Tyrone. "But that motherfucker don't own this place. I don't give a fuck what he say. I pay my motherfuckin' rent for this room, and I can smoke in my god-damn room if I want to. Fuck him—he's got those rules posted up in the kitchen there. I don't see how you and Ray go on outside all the motherfuckin' time. I guess you're just law abiding or something. 'Cause I don't give a motherfuck. And what's the motherfucker gon' do. The motherfucker ain't kickin' no one's ass, least of alls mine. The way he always motherfuckin' talkin' like he's some kind of tough guy or something. Motherfucker give me a motherfuckin' break. I'll put a bullet in his ass right quick like a motherfucker." He bugged his eyes out and stretched and realigned his jaw. He dug at the back of his neck with his nails. "Whew, motherfucker," he said, sweating. His glasses were crooked on his face, but he did not bother to move them. He squinted at Zero out of his right eye through the left lens.

"Now I been shooting dope for more than twenty motherfuckin' years Zero, and I'll be shooting it till the day I motherfuckin' die, if I can help it.... And I always had me a motherfuckin' job.... I started down on the corner of 138th Street and Amstermotherfuckin'dam Avenue in Nuevamotherfuckin'York.... There ain't nothing I like better than some of this dicksuckin' motherfuckin' good hair-on. I'll stay like this all motherfuckin' day long...." His head fell to his chest.

Zero fumbled through his pockets. He felt the ocean inside him swelling up, getting larger, stronger. Things slowed down all around him. He pulled at his nose. "Throw me a cigarette there, Tttyyyrrrooonnneee...."

Tyrone half opened an eye. He absentmindedly reached over to the nightstand for his cigarettes. He worked one of them out of the package from his position on the bed and lobbed it across the room.

Zero reached for it, missing. He bent down. The lighter fell in front of him. He picked them both up. He stuck a crumpled cigarette in his mouth and struck the flint on the plastic lighter.

Tyrone said, "Throw me the *TV Guide* over there, Zero

man, so I can see if they got a good motherfuckin' war movie or something on." He rubbed at the scar on the inside of his elbow, blinked his eyes open, and turned to the nightstand. He rummaged through the empty Thunderbird bottles and overflowing ashtrays, finding his cigarette still burning on the wood surface. He picked it up from off of the blackened spot and sucked on it, feeling good.

Zero was feeling warmer, his pores opening up to sweat, droplets beginning to form. "Hey, this shit is all right," he said. He reached down to a pile of newspapers on the floor, nearly falling out of his seat. He took the *TV Guide*, dropped it, then picked it up again. He sat up, sweating. "No problem," he said, tossing the booklet toward Tyrone. The pages flapped in the air.

Tyrone poked around inside the nightstand drawer, uncovering a tube of ointment. He squeezed some out onto his fingertips and began rubbing his wound with it. He shut his eyes, his mouth wide open.

Zero had his cigarette in the lighter flame. His eyes were closed.

Tyrone snapped out of it. He wiped the drool from the corner of his mouth. He said, "Shit, I'm sitting here sucking my own motherfuckin' dick." He picked his head up off his chest and looked across the room to Zero. "You gon' burn the whole motherfuckin' house down. Hey, Zero!" shouted Tyrone.

Zero came to. His face was in the growing flame. Half the

cigarette was deeply blackened, and it now burned in more than one place. He could not feel the heat from the lighter.

"Say, how 'bout if I make something to eat," said Tyrone. He lifted his head off his chest to say this. The cigarette filter burned the skin on his fingers. He crushed it out in the ashtray, then rearranged the erection in his pants.

"Doesn't matter to me," said Zero. He felt nauseated. He got up off the chair, warmer and sweating. He stretched out on the floor of the room. "Whatever you make's all right with me," he said from the floor. He folded his arms for a pillow and rested his head on them, then he closed his eyes.

"Say, how 'bout if I make something to eat," said Tyrone. He opened an eye and peeked at Zero. "Don't plan on dying right there on the floor," he said. "You ain't getting no motherfuckin' funeral if you do. In this state they're gon' put my black ass in the motherfuckin' penitentiary if they find a dead body in my room. It don't matter what, or who, or why.... Your ass be dumped in the ocean if anything like that happen. I feel sorry for your family, but they ought to know with a dope fiend in the house that anything is liable to happen.... I spent all my motherfuckin' life trying to stay out of the penitentiary, and your ass dying off a little dope ain't gon' put me there either."

On the floor Zero lay there smiling at the warmth and color behind his eyelids.

Some days later there was the smell of fire in the air. Zero walked down the Boulevard on his way home from work and looking up could see black smoke in the western sky ahead of him. He had got off the bus at an earlier stop than usual, Calle 25, so he could stop at the Liquor Locker. It was the only place he knew of in town where he could buy cans of Snappy Tom tomato and chili cocktail drinks. When they were out of the Snappy Toms, Zero bought the Hot and Spicy V-8s, and when they were out of both he bought the regular V-8 and added his own drops of Tabasco to it. He kept the cans at room temperature on the floor of his room. It was dark and dank enough in there, and when it did warm up that was fine with him also, because he especially liked his tomato and chili drinks warm, the way he liked his malt liquor. He knew if he left them in the refrigerator in the kitchen they would be gone before long without a trace, even though all of the other five residents of the house claimed not to like the flavor.

Zero carried six cans of Snappy Tom in a bag. The air outside the Liquor Locker was dry. It was ninety degrees in July. On the radio earlier they had said it was the hottest day of the year so far. He started to walk the fifteen blocks to Calle 10. He looked up ahead into the western sky. It was orange- and purple-shaded from the sun setting over the bay. A column of black smoke rose over the Boulevard in the distance. One moment it looked like it was dissipating, the next it was again growing. He could not tell whether it came from somewhere south of the Boulevard near his house, or north of it near the oil refinery. Today no breeze blew off of the bay.

As he passed City Park he heard small explosions coming from out of a grove of trees. When he first moved to the city both Henry and Tyrone had referred to the place as Loco Park and warned him, "Don't go in the park after dark, and in the day only if you're gay." Whether it was kids shooting off firecrackers left over from the 4th of July or kids shooting at each other with .22s, Zero was not going to check for certain. He kept straight on the Boulevard.

Most of the buildings along the street were one-story, stucco, glass-fronted office buildings and store fronts. There was a motorcycle parts distributor and right next door a bar frequented by bikers. There were a total of five bars and four liquor stores between Zero and home. Near the Civic Center, where the police station and city hall were, lawyers and bail bondsmen had set up offices. A couple of the corners were occupied by drive-thru, national fast-food chain restaurants with lines of cars overflowing the parking lots. Uptown Billiards and Bowling had a giant top hat and cane painted on the side of the building. The wall was crowded with gang graffiti and bullet holes. Between Calle 23 and 22 there was a row of beauty parlors and manicure salons. During the off hours the pretty Asian women workers dressed in miniskirts and with their hair teased high gathered in the doorways. Zero thought it looked like a Bangkok red-light district and could not imagine the workers were not baking their brains with the chemicals they inhaled all day long while they worked, no matter that they wore surgical masks.

At the house on Calle 10 the rent was cheap enough for

Zero to afford. He brought home from work a little more than two hundred dollars a week. When he moved in Henry said to him, "The rent is fifty bucks a week. Or else I can let you have it for two hundred dollars a month, since we been knowing each other for so long, carnal. And your father was Chicano and my sister is Chicana, and you're Chicano and my mother is Chicana, and your brother is Chicano and so am I. Chicano."

Zero did not know what Henry had meant, but said, "I'll take the two hundred dollars a month deal."

Henry said to him, "It would be very beneficiary for you to do so."

The low rent allowed Zero to pay off some of the credit card companies and collection agencies who had been hounding him and searching for him after years of drinking and irresponsibility. Before he graduated from college in a drunken blur he applied for as many credit cards as he could get his hands on, and much to his surprise they all were approved, offering him several thousand dollars worth of credit each. He ended up using the cards only when he was drunk, and he rarely remembered to keep track of the debt or send in the payment. In a matter of months he had gone the limit on all of the cards and they were taken away, leaving him in a ten-thousand-dollar-deep hole. For a while he tried his best to keep up with the payments, but it never lasted long. When the letters came in the mail he would tear them up or just not bother to open them. When they phoned him he hung up on them. When they came knocking at his door he refused to answer it. Before long the debts had all become delinquent. And when his landlady asked him to vacate the premises he never bothered putting in a change of address with the post office, so none of the bills was ever forwarded. During his drunk years Zero changed his residence often to stay ahead of landlords. He didn't spend much time worrying about creditors.

When he stopped drinking he stopped running. These days if they caught up with him he made arrangements to pay off the debt in installments. These he stuck to as well as possible. He paid them back as a somewhat perverse sense of reward for finding him. He knew they had to be doing their jobs extraordinarily well to have tracked him down. All his life he had been trained to run. And so, though the credit cards had long ago been taken away, the debt remained, and grew from the interest.

Henry kept telling Zero he should consolidate all his bills into one monthly payment. "That's what I'm gonna do, bro'," he said.

Zero thought it was just fine the way it was now. If they find me, okay, I will then begin to pay them back. If no one will ever rent me an apartment because of my bad credit history, that's okay also. He would not have to worry about it while he lived in Ciudad Jimenez.

Henry then said to Zero, "Hey, bro', do me a favor and write down that old credit card number. Do you still know it? I could get some shit for free on that number. Since you got it settled with them, and are paying it off and everything, they ain't gonna suspect you 'bout nothing. This mallate taught me this scam when I was in the jailhouse a couple of years back. It makes sense to me, bro'. And I'll tell you, I thought of something like this myself once before that mallate ever told me nothing."

From Calle 20 down to the waterfront the streets and sidewalks were littered with broken glass, used condoms, discarded hypodermic needles, and dog crap. Zero sniffed at the air. There was the smell of rubber or something similar burning. He thought it might be the refinery.

The Jimenez Refinery played a major role in the development of the city. It occupied a 3500-acre parcel of land in the northwesternmost corner of the city with the bay surrounding it on the north and west. Many of the housing developments in the city were built to accommodate the ever-growing work force needed by the refinery. As the refinery grew, the city grew and became more dirty and crowded. At one time a majority of the city residents either worked there in some capacity or another or had a friend or family member who did. Now the jobs were filled mostly by residents of the adjoining suburban cities east of Ciudad Jimenez.

And the refinery no longer contributed as it once had seemed to the development and prosperity of the city. The cancer rate among Ciudad Jimenez residents grew exponentially in relation to the distance a person lived from the refinery. Children who grew up near it had a high incidence of developing respiratory problems as they got older.

A daily stench rose from the smokestacks and blew across the city. Sometimes clouds of toxic chemicals were released into the atmosphere by accident. Refinery spokesmen on television would later deny the accident took place or downplay the danger, no matter that groups of citizens had been treated at local hospitals complaining of eye irritation and vomiting. Most residents of the city Zero had met, both lifelong and transplanted, expressed a fear and knowledge that one day the Jimenez Refinery would blow up and make the Bhopal disaster of the mid-1980s look like a picnic in the sun.

Zero took a breath and held it for as long as he could. The smell of rubber burning grew stronger. One day a few months back Ray sat with Zero in his room smoking grass when they noticed outside the window, in the distance, smoke rising from a fire. They both tried to guess the intersection that was burning. And later that afternoon they drove to the liquor store, passing closer to the billowing clouds of black smoke and learning it was a paint company that burned. The two sped on back to the house while sirens rushed past them. On the television that night the newscaster said the fire had burned for forty-five minutes, releasing a toxic cloud all the while, before fire officials had been called.

Zero let his breath out. Up ahead he could see three police squad cars with their lights flashing crowded in the parking lot and on the sidewalk of the Jalisco Bar at Calle 19. One of the workers from el taco truck held a long metal bar in his hands. The officers searched two suspects bent over the hood of a car. Zero changed his plans for dinner and headed for the underpass. He took another breath and held it.

The column of black smoke rose above the backyard of the house on Calle 10. From the vacant lot next door Zero could hear loud, drunken voices as he approached the house. He could also make out shapes, though barely discernible, behind a plastic green mesh hanging over the wire fence. It looked like several men stood around the BBQ pit: a fifty-five-gallon oil drum lying on its side and welded to a stand on wheels with the top portion cut away. Henry's primo, Larry, had made it for him as a gift half a dozen years ago. Flames jumped up above the height of the fence. Through the clamor Zero recognized the thick-accented voice of Pancho from the room next door to his own, Tyrone's laughter, and Ray's howling from the other side of the yard near the Pontiac. One of the men spotted Zero, and they all started calling:

"Hey! Come on over here. Now, man!"

"Eh, Zzzeeerrrooo! Oooooowwwwww!"

"All right!"

"Zzzzzzeeeeeerrrrrroooooo!"

"Oooooowwwwww!"

"You got any weed?"

Zero waved to the fence of voices, knowing they could see him through the mesh, and headed for the front door. It was difficult to open. He had to push against it several times before he could finally get inside.

En la entrada he saw that two boys' motocross bikes had

been leaned up against the door. He noticed a couple of large, gray, plastic garbage bags also piled up in the small, dark space. He kicked one of them. It sounded and felt like it was filled with wet clothes. Increasingly, these bags had been crowding the way into the house. The bags were filled with wet clothes waiting to be dried. Others contained dirty and smelly clothes waiting to be washed. Henry, these days, seemed always to be doing laundry even though his boys were there only two weekends out of the month and on some mornings before school.

The washer and dryer belonged to Henry. He let no one else in the house use them, saying, "Eh, if it breaks down on you, you ain't gonna wanna pay to fix it." He had salvaged the appliances from his marriage. During the divorce proceedings they were some of the few items he could convince the judge to let him have. Henry said, "That bitch don't know nothing 'bout no clean clothes anyway, homes. I don't know how I could have standed it for so many years."

In the hallway Zero ran into Henry walking out of the bathroom.

"Eh, I didn't go to work today, ese," said Henry. He had a glazed, cross-eyed look in his eyes. "Did they ask for me?" He lumbered about in the hallway and drank from a can of malt liquor.

"Nobody asked me," said Zero. "What's going on?"

Henry spoke and burped at the same time, "Fffuuuccckkk-eeeddd uuuppp." He smiled at his own cleverness. "Come on outside, bro'. We got some food on the grill still, I think."

Zero moved to the side to let Henry pass.

Henry went by, then turned and asked, "Eh, you got any herb?"

"I got a little bit. I'll be out in a while," said Zero.

Henry smiled and leaned a shoulder against the wall, relaxing. He was dressed in a light green polyester running suit, worn thin from the years. His sneakers were full of holes. He let out a deep breath. "Eh, you got any of those coloradas? Pills, ese? That shit was good," said Henry. He picked at his groin. "I saw you las' night, bro'. Was you drinking? You looked pretty buzzed." He drank from his malt liquor.

"Dope," said Zero. In fact it had not been the night before, but several days ago. The lethargy from the narcotics only lasted for one day afterward. He felt none of it yesterday or today. It was not worth the effort to explain all this to Henry. Zero saw that look in his eyes that meant Henry would probably not remember this day.

"Did you do it?" asked Henry, motioning as if he was injecting something into his arm.

"El naris," said Zero.

"Yo soy," said Henry.

"It was pretty good," said Zero.

"Oh yeah, ese?" said Henry. He moved in a little closer and lowered his voice. "Eh, let me know the next time you gonna be getting some more of that. All right? But don't tell you-know-who." Henry stepped back some and mouthed the words *el mallate* to Zero. He pointed to the backyard.

"Yeah. All right," said Zero. He moved his package from one arm to the other.

"Eh, you got beer in there, ese?" asked Henry. He finished

his drink and put the empty can in a plastic garbage bag. "We gotta keep this place tidy," he said. He stumbled backwards a little into a stack of three boxes, his and his boys' possessions, in the hallway. "Whoa," he said, catching himself.

"Tomato and chili drink," said Zero.

"Ugh," said Henry. He stuck out a gray-colored tongue in disgust. "You ain't gonna put that in the refrigerator is you?"

"No, I wasn't going to," said Zero. "I'll see you outside."

"Okay, bro'," said Henry, not moving. There were dirt streaks on the side of his face. "That bitch came by earlier and took the boys," he said. He wiped more dirt and sweat across his forehead. The glare in his eyes grew deeper. "It was some crazy shit, I'm telling you," he said.

"Okay. I'll see you," said Zero, this time not waiting for Henry to leave first. He turned and went down the hallway to the back of the house.

The air was stifling inside his room. He placed the bag of drinks in the middle of the floor, then he moved out of his way a small black-and-white television that sat on top of a red, plastic milk crate. He sat down at the foot of the bed, reached up, and opened a window. He closed it immediately when he realized there was still something horrible smelling and probably toxic burning on the BBQ grill. His shirt was stuck to his back now, and sweat dripped down from his chin. He made sure the curtains were closed and noticed that the walls on that side of the room, like all the others, were full of mold.

The mold was out of control in his room, especially on the

wall behind the head of the bed. He had cleaned it off twice before, but it always came back. Now he waited for Henry to make good on the promise of painting the room to help alleviate the problem. Sometimes Henry would say to Zero, "Eh, I don't know what you do, but that shit looks real nasty." Zero would answer him, "Man, I need to get pinche management off their ass and to work."

The floor boards were warped and uneven in the room, bent up now from the moisture. In the room there was also the odd odor of living, breathing, and growing fungus.

In an offhand manner Henry tried to blame it all on Zero, though they both knew the walls were that way before he moved in. Henry always made remarks to Zero about cleaning up around the house. Zero kept the door to his room closed and every month tried to remember to clean the bathtub and sink, which was his one chore. Everyone in the house had something to do. Zero didn't know what else Henry expected of him. Long ago he had stopped using the kitchen because of the filth.

"And you can clean up around here, too," Henry would say. "You know what I'm talkin' 'bout, ese?"

Zero didn't know what Henry was talking about and thought he already did his share by putting up with the clutter all around him and, more often than not, paying his rent on time.

Outside in the yard Henry's dog, Tangerine, was barking. Zero was glad the days were gone when the bitch had her litter underneath his room. For two weeks there she nursed the puppies. Most of those days and nights the little animals whimpered and cried while Tangerine was out running around in the streets. Finally, Henry gave them all away and claimed there was nothing he could have done about it. "You know how the bitches are about those things, ese," said Henry.

Zero leaned back on the folding bed, moving clothes and newspapers out of the way. It was the first time in years he had lived with a bed. It was already here when he rented the room. In the past it had not been cheap enough or important enough for him to go out and buy a bed. He didn't mind sleeping on the floor after a while, which was good since he had no other choice. Now he slept in two sleeping bags, zipped up, one inside the other, on top of the mattress. There were no sheets. He did have a pillow, though he didn't know where it came from. It was a novelty for him to be so far up in the air on the folding frame.

He pulled his shirt off, still lying there, and in doing so banged his wrist on his ghetto blaster, which was set atop another plastic milk crate there at the head of the bed. It was nothing too fancy or large, but it had a cassette player and AM/FM radio. The speakers were supposed to detach, though he had never tried to take them off. His family en El Sur had sent the thing to him about a year ago.

On the wall opposite Zero was a freestanding, gray metal shelving unit. The unit leaned toward the back of the house because of the weight of the clothes, newspapers, and books on the three shelves. Zero stood and walked over to it. He noticed he could hear the evening news on the television in Pancho's room on the other side of the wall. The television seemed to always be on in there, and Zero learned to tune out the noise, most of the time.

He pushed a pair of jeans out of the way to clear a space on the top shelf. A few paperback books fell off, and he bent over to pick them up. Zero grabbed the first book, *The Cool World*, by Warren Miller. He remembered he had seen the black-and-white movie adaptation of the novel before he had ever known there was a book. The next book was *Blue Day on Main Street*, by J. L. Navarro, an author whose stories he first came across in the East Los Angeles magazine, *Con Safos*. He put these two on the bottom shelf. The third book was *Barrabas*, by Par Lagervist. Zero thought about Barrabas. Jesus Christ really died for that man's sins. He tossed the book onto the bed, planning to reread it.

Zero heard shouts coming from the backyard like there was a fight, but it quickly changed to peaceful howling. Zero reached into his left pocket and pulled out a crumpled ten-dollar bill and his keys. On the key ring he saw the keys his mother had given him when he was a child. He still used them on the rare occasion that he visited his family. He once had the keys to La Wilma's apartment also, but no more. Zero straightened out the bill. In the other pocket he found three singles and sixty-three cents. He put the two quarters back in his pocket; he dropped the dime and pennies in an empty beer can he used as a bank on the second shelf. He remembered when he was sixteen years old he used a round oatmeal carton as a coin bank. He and his then buddy, Roberto, carried it to the Food King a few times when they were zombies on a PCP-dipped cigarette, a Sherman, and dumped the coins out onto the counter in exchange for bills, enough to get another seven-dollar-and-fifty-cent piece.

Zero took two of the dollar bills and walked to his dresser in the corner near his closet. The dresser was small with two drawers at the top and two at the bottom. There was cabinet space in between, with two doors opening out. On top of the dresser there were several copies of *MAD* magazine and *Pro Wrestling Illustrated*. He thought they had something in common, but was not sure what that something was. He sometimes wondered what the lives of the people who worked at those publications were like: the constant blood, sweat, and physical pain of the cartoon world.

In a bottom dresser drawer filled with socks, t-shirts, and boxer shorts, Zero kept a folded lunch bag with money in it. He tried to save two dollars a day, but he remembered to only four or five times out of a week. In the bag there was nearly forty dollars. Hidden in the closet he had a hundred-dollar bill. He was saving the money for something, though he did not yet know what he wanted. He could not remember ever saving more than the three hundred dollars he had had when he was eighteen and left home for the university.

Back at the shelf he put the rest of the bills in his wallet. From out of a back pocket he took out some folded flyers a man had handed him when he was walking around downtown Oakland during his lunch break. One flyer was a coupon for a free chiropractic examination. The other one advertised a sale of three porno videotapes for ten dollars. Zero was saving it for Ray. He discovered he also had a box cutter in the pocket.

At work he had slipped it in there after using it earlier in the day and then forgotten about it and brought it home. Zero thought about one of his bosses: screw that stupid, rich bitch Sarah Miller from La Frontera en El Sur. She can lick my ass clean with her job. And she's not as fine as she thinks, he thought. Zero was reassured that even her husband and business associates could not stand her, and everyone else in the shop hated to work with her. Any day she was not in the building was considered by all almost a holiday.

The woman did not have the sense enough to stay home or realize the company ran best when she was not around and meddling in the work of her employees. She was supposed to bring new printing jobs into the shop, but with her caustic personality she was not very good at that. At the shop she mostly cursed at her husband and business associates over the phone, calling them idiots, and she herself wanted the least of all to do with her employees. She sometimes wished they were her personal slaves, especially the black stud, Leroy, who cleaned up around the shop.

Other times the woman would be bored and would try to help by answering the company telephone. When she tired of that she would have the bright idea to clean up around the shop and rearrange the stock in the warehouse, which always meant Leroy and Zero moving pallets and giant reams, cartons, and boxes of paper around, from location to location, while Sarah tried to decide where they looked better. Zero had accidentally found out through the company files that her father really owned the business. Sarah claimed to have built Company Printing up from nothing. Zero told everyone in the shop what he had learned about her.

Zero did not like the idea of carrying a knife. In one of his jackets hanging in the closet he kept a small, half-inch-thick steel bar. It was seven inches long; he had found it one day, shining in the middle of an intersection. It was a solid weapon, and he had kept it in the inside breast pocket of the jacket ever since. He was not sure what the police would do if they found it on him. The last time he had been stopped and searched he, luckily, had not been wearing that jacket. He was sure he would be in trouble if the police found the box cutter on him. They would never believe he had a job, let alone that he used the razor for cutting open boxes at his job. Zero imagined a smart-ass police officer saying to him, "You work as a slasher, right?" before the man brought out his handcuffs.

As a child en El Sur there were times before when he had carried a knife. He was grateful that he had never had to use it or pull it out on anyone. For more than half his life, now, he had been walking the streets and riding the buses of big cities and, most times, that was a dangerous activity. Once when he was eleven years old he had fought with a stick. It was not that he had intended to use it—he just happened to be carrying one when the fight started on the street corner. The same when he was a teenager and beat someone with an umbrella in the pouring rain. And one time he had his jaw broken when he was jumped by a group of four.

He went over to the closet and looked inside. There were ten boxes stacked three and four high, filled mostly with notebooks and papers left over from the years he spent at the university. He had studied sociology. The more he learned and understood about society, the less, it seemed, he wanted anything to do with it.

He took the second box from the top from a stack in the corner and carried it to the middle of the room. When he first moved into the house on Calle 10, Zero paid Henry ten dollars to drive him over to the rental storage space to pick up these boxes. Henry kept complaining over and over about how early it was in the morning, how hungry he was, and that he had charged a homeboy fifteen dollars the weekend before to do almost the same thing. So Zero took him out to breakfast at Bongo Burgers where for a dollar and a half they served two eggs any style, homefries, and toast. Zero liked the homefries especially because they were loaded with onions and green peppers. And the price was so reasonable that sometimes Zero could afford not only to treat himself but a friend also. Zero had been coming here for years. The place was near the university.

He had done well enough in school. All his life he had been able to get along with a minimum of studying and still come out with a B average, give or take a few grade points, even during the eight drunken years of college. And he still read books, mostly novels.

Zero grabbed his chair and put it near the box. He leaned over and pulled a notebook from out of it. On the cover was written: POLITICAL SOCIOLOGY 151. He opened it up and read a page:

> ... researchers disclose that the richest 1 percent of the households in this country held/owned 37 percent of the country's total private wealth.... The richest 10 percent of the population held 68 percent of the nation's private assets—stocks, bonds, real estate, personal property, bank deposits, and ownership. The remaining 90 percent of the population/nation's households owned 32 percent of individual wealth....

Zero wanted to smoke a cigarette. He could still hear the voices outside in the backyard, but he did not want to join them yet. He turned to another page and read:

> ... a conscious effort has been made to determine how the majority of our tax dollars is spent.... And how the government influences society ... a conscious choice between guns and butter ... the social justice agenda has all but been eliminated through cuts in social programs that benefit the poor and the redirection of those monies....

There was a fly buzzing around Zero's head. He swatted at it, wondering how it had gotten inside. He looked up at it as it flew away, too far out of reach on the ceiling. He took a quick glance around the room to see if there were others, then reached down to the bag on the floor and opened a Snappy Tom to drink.

Something fell out of the pages of the notebook. It was a Polaroid snapshot. Zero picked it up and looked at it. The date scratched on it in fading blue ink was September 16. He still remembered the day.

He had just turned eighteen, and it was the day he left home for El Norte. It was that evening, and he had gone down the street to say good-bye to his friends and to have one last beer and smoke of yesca before leaving.

The group in the photo looked more lost than tough. One of the boys was not even a friend of his: just another hoodlum from down the street to take his place among the group of them. Zero had not seen any of those in the photo for years. And he had no reason to believe he ever would again.

Zero took a drink of the tomato and chili flavor. Back then when the photo was taken the only gabachos Zero knew of were on television, his teachers, and in police uniforms. The world he lived in was nothing like theirs.

His father, so the story goes, had once been a zoot-suiter. The man died when Zero was still in high school. He came home one day to find him face down on the kitchen floor where he had fallen from a not-so-quiet overdose of Percodan and whiskey. Zero had been outraged to learn the man had been on dope and had searched the house looking for any leftover pills, but much to his disappointment nothing turned up.

Zero himself had followed in the long family tradition of poverty and alcoholism. And who could say for certain that his father's overdose had been an accident? Suicide had been on Zero's mind for as long as he could remember.

As a child Zero had once said to his mother, "Mama, I walk around with the barrio in my head." He was a lanky little boy whose arms seemed too long for the rest of his body. And the woman looked at him not knowing what he was talking about. Only a few days earlier Zero had stood at the front screen door and watched, in the sunlight of a Saturday afternoon, the street and sidewalks fill up with Chicanos of all shapes and sizes and shades of brown, marching past his house and shouting for an end to the killings.

His mother had come up behind him after a few minutes of standing there. The street still was crowded, the stream of dark faces moving steadily by. "Don't pay attention to those gang members," said his mother, closing the door.

The nine-year-old Zero did not agree with his mother. He thought, They all look like me, my brothers, sisters, mother, and father, but he could never say this out loud.

As a man he still made the effort to walk around with the barrio in his head: the knowledge that he had been born of dirt and would someday return to dirt. He was born in the barrio and would die in it, he knew. And on a street corner, more than likely, when he was thirty-five or forty-three, or tomorrow; he did not know how many times already he had escaped the confinement of a long pine box.

One day when Zero and Ray were sitting in the sala

sharing a tokiaso, the pipe smoking, passing back and forth between the two of them, and the sweet smell of yesca filling the house, Ray said, "I am el cabron fat loco. Gordito locito, yo soy!" and punched his fist in the air.

Zero only smiled at him, holding the smoke in his lungs.

Ray went on, "Eh, isn't that weird that you don't know when you will die." Ray shook visibly. "Eh, you know, ese, that scared me when I said that. Like maybe I shouldn't have. You know what I'm saying, ese? You don't never know when it's gonna happen. It just does.... Just like when you first become conscious of being alive. It just happens, que no, ese? It could happen now!" Ray bugged his eyes out as he said this. "...Or now!" Ray clutched his hand to his chest in a mock heart attack. He closed his left eye as the smoke from the pipe curled past it, then Ray smiled. "I'm telling you, I don't know what it means, ese, but it's just like when you realize you are here. Alive! man. When does that happen? Just one day you begin to remember from day to day. You begin to think, though you must have been doing that before, now you remember it. You notice you are here." Ray stood and moved his body to his left. "And your family is over there." Ray pointed to where he had been standing, then moved back to his right. "And then you realize there is a world of people out there other than your family and yourself." Ray became quiet, smoking the pipe in silence for a moment. Then he began again, "Eh, Zero I don't wanna tell you exactly how old I am 'cause you will think I'm some kind of viejo or something, but I will tell you that I'm now past forty. Believe me.... And I'll tell you sometimes it don't feel no different than when I was nineteen or twenty. Sometimes … like when I'm out in the Valley and that fat broad is sucking on my dick … ooh la la … you know what I'm saying, ese?" Ray swirled his hips in a circle lewdly. "Ooh la la," he said, then sat back down.

"Fuck you, ooh la la," said Zero, reaching over and taking the pipe out of Ray's mouth. "You've got to pass this thing back to me."

As he sat there Zero thought back to his first memory. In it he is not quite four years old and standing in front of the house en El Sur. If there are any of his family around at that time he is unaware of it. Nor does he remember it now or fabricate a memory of it. In the years since he sometimes wondered if this first memory itself had been fabricated somewhere sometime in his own imagination; maybe it had been a dream, but the memory, the images, they had all been with him now for more than twenty years, and where would have been the profit or motivation for the young Zero to make up those images that had always disturbed him? The jeeps and trucks that he had seen that morning filled with soldiers while he looked four lots down to the corner where they traveled in a long line heading west, some of them with their rifles pointing toward the houses. Later he learned through newspaper clippings he found in the attic that they were National Guardsmen sent in by the government during the times of the riots.

He was fourteen years old when he first started smoking weed. A couple of months later he was selling joints for fifty cents a piece to the other ninth graders. He kept them hidden in a folded bandana in his back pocket. He would begin with ten or twenty in the morning and by noon he would have none. He would peddle them in the hallway between classes, would even duck into the waiting area outside the dean's office on occasion to roll up a bomber for Ronnie, special because they had gone to grammar school together and lived in the same barrio.

And shortly before his father died Zero apologized to his mother one time when he was drunk. It was the first sign that he would someday drink like his father. His mother continually slapped him; back and forth went his head, crying and stuttering and slobbering his words. Those slaps were the last time she ever touched him.

He had already thrown up once all over the living room floor and snot rolled on long slinky globs hanging out of his nostrils in the air. She had scolded him earlier in the day not to go out to the protest with those gang members who she knew were always causing trouble with the police and the authorities downtown, and had been since the 1940s when she was a teenager, and even before, she knew, because she had grown up in this city.

Zero had said, "Lo siento, mama, pero yo soy Chicano tambien." He then went stumbling into the bathroom, too late though and just missing the toilet bowl, retching on the floor over and over, a river of lumpy tortilla chips and apple-flavored Night Train wine spreading across the tile floor.

Zero slipped the Polaroid into his back pocket. He could hear a bottle break outside, then another. He paused for a moment, then stood up and went to the window. More glass broke amid shouts. Zero halted before pulling back the curtain. He heard:

"Eh, what's going on? Fucker!"

There was laughter, then muffled shouts of a scuffle. Zero went back to his seat. He reached down to the bottom of the box and found two prescription bottles there.

After much argument with Sarah at work, Zero had gotten her to give him health insurance. He still had to pay a portion of the cost himself out of his wages because he only worked thirty-two and not forty hours per week. It was still worth the effort. His wisdom teeth had been bothering him for more than a year. And he had two broken teeth: one from a couple of years earlier when he took a dive down a flight of concrete stairs after washing down a handful of valiums with a pint of tequila; the other was from his first year in college. He and two other friends were jumped by ten white fraternity boys at a party. Zero and his friends were too young and stupid to know that it made no difference they were all students at the same university and thought no one would notice that they were Chicanos. On top of it all, Zero had no cavities. And had scored three times on some narcotics.

He remembered with relish the prescription being handed over to him the first time. In an act of boldness Zero had come right out and said specifically to the dentist not to give him any Codeine Number 3s, because, he said, they didn't work. He really wanted something stronger.

The dentist stopped what he was doing. "What do you mean?" he asked.

Zero was still lying back some in the chair, not facing the dentist. Still, he was glad his face was numb from the Novocaine. He tried to look serious, but also like it did not matter if he were given anything at all. "I had my jaw broken a couple of years ago. And they gave me that. But it didn't really work," he said.

The dentist seemed astonished that Zero could speak about his broken jaw with such ease. "Okay. All right," he said. "I'll give you some Vicodin. It ought to work all right. It's a synthetic codeine, similar to a Number 4. You should be fine."

"Okay, I guess," said Zero. "Anything that's going to take the pain away."

The dentist glanced up from the prescription tablet and looked Zero dead center in the eyes. "Is there much pain?" he asked.

"Oh yeah," said Zero, curling his toes to keep from breaking into a big smile. "It hurts a lot."

"Well, this should do the trick. And we'll see you again in a couple of weeks for that root canal." The dentist gave Zero the prescription and extended his hand.

Zero left the building in a hurry, trying to make it to a pharmacy before they closed. It was almost 5 PM. There was one right around the corner, but they wanted him to pick the pills up in the morning, and there was no way he was going to part with the slip of paper without getting some narcotics in return.

He got thirty pills the first time and twenty on the subsequent visit, fifty in all. It took three or four of them for Zero to feel stupid the way he wanted to, so low down it felt like his dick would fall off his body. Both times when he came home Henry was there waiting and asked Zero if he had got anything, and Zero would say, "Not really. I just got a little bit. You know they didn't wanna give me even this much. Because they see a Chicano and figure: drug addict."

When he went to the oral surgeon for his impacted wisdom teeth, Zero got a little greedy, asking for Percodan specifically. This time the dentist didn't buy the story about the broken jaw, even though it was true.

"Didn't you say you had a drug problem?" he asked Zero, pulling off his rubber gloves and peering at him over the tops of his bifocals.

Zero tried not to look disappointed. "No. That was an alcohol problem," he said.

Eventually the man wrote the prescription for some Demerol, and much to Zero's later surprise, the pharmacist made a mistake and gave him thirty pills instead of twenty-five. As he stood at the bus stop Zero gobbled two of them, but was impatient. He had never had Demerol before, and he started feeling cheated because they were taking so long to kick in. He stepped into a bookstore nearby and looked the drug up in the *PDR*. It said synthetic morphine. Zero thought, Righteous! And slipped two more pills into his mouth as he sat waiting.

They worked just right, laying him out on the bus before he was halfway home. He was leaning way over in his seat, drooling and trying to keep upright. He scratched lazily when he straightened up.

The next day he again got greedy, taking twice as many because the same dosage from the day before wasn't working. After that he waited a few weeks before taking any more, and when he did they laid him out, almost dead he was so unconscious, on his back all over again. And he loved it. Zero was very pleased with his health insurance. And he also liked the fact that he had Sarah Miller to thank for it all. Her and her generosity, he thought.

He had been saving the pills for a while, stretching them out for as long as he could. He waited a month, then took four more and visited the dead again. He would take three or four at a time, waiting weeks or months in between. He was now left with only five, which he was saving for a special occasion.

The last of his supply of drugs was some five milligram capsules of Valium his partner Joe had smuggled to him from Mexico. Joe had bought them at the farmacia like aspirin, he told Zero. And Zero loved that country even more because of it, even though he had never been there.

He didn't have many pills left. And all his dental work had been completed. There were still ninety milligrams of the

Valium left. He could either take it all at once for a real good time or split it into two doses and take it before work for kicks. He would have to remember to ask Joe if he had anymore, the next time he spoke to him.

The group outside in the yard began shouting:

"Eh, ese, what happened to Zero and that joint?"

"Yeah. What happened to that vato? Did he skip out on us?"

"Say, whyn't one of you all motherfuckers go over and tap on his motherfuckin' window and wake his motherfuckin' ass up."

"Maybe the motherfucker went and overdosed, or something."

"Eh, check it out, ese. I bet he's in there pulling his pud, or something, man."

"Oh yeah. And you want to watch, huh?"

"Let's check it out."

Zero scooped the pills all back into the bottles and stuffed them into the bottom of the box, piling notebooks and papers on top of them. He could hear the group of voices getting closer as he stood and replaced the box to the stack in the closet. He heard the group right outside his window when he stepped out of the room.

In the hallway he ran into Ray.

"Eh, carnal," said Ray. "How you doing man, all right? Man, listen to me, man. Listen to me, man...." Ray lowered his voice conspiratorially. "Listen here, man. Listen here," he said, "I'm fucked up, man. I'm telling you. I'm fucked up. I been here all day, homes. Man, we been having a good-ass time. You know what I'm saying, ese? But listen to me, man. Listen to me. I'm fucked up…. Hey, how you been anyway? Come on outside, man, don't be shy. Where you been all day? I been here since morning. Drinking. Toking. Hey, you got anymore of those pills, ese? You was all fucked up the other night. I know that shit was good. You was fffeeeeeellliiinnnggg gggooooooooddd." Ray started walk-ing back up the hallway. "Eh, wait, man," he said, stopping. "Listen to me, man. I'm fucked up. Come on outside, man. We're getting fucked up all day long." Ray began walking out of the house, through the hallway, to the kitchen, through to the laundry room.

Zero followed him. Ray stopped at the back door before going outside. He said, "Man, I fell asleep in the sun out there, homes. I'm all burned up. I passed out at 12 noon, homes, and woke up at 3 PM. I been drinking all day long. I seen you earlier in the morning…. Where you been all day?"

PART III

At work Sarah would not concede. She and Zero stood in a far corner of the cavernous warehouse space. It was a hundred feet across and twice as long. From the other side of the room came the faint sound of Salsa music from a radio near Henry's printing press. In the background was the constant ka-chink ka-chink sound of a larger press running. The pair stood among boxes of paper.

"You realize we didn't have to let you have the health coverage," said the woman to Zero. She scowled at him as if he was a dirty, foul-mouthed, trouble-making third-grade pervert who, once again, was in the principal's office when he ought to have been in juvenile hall already. If it was up to her, he would be.

"I realize that," said Zero.

"Look at me when I talk to you," said Sarah.

Zero turned toward her but did not make eye contact. He looked over her left shoulder. On the other side of the warehouse Henry and Leroy made obscene gestures behind the woman's back.

Beside Henry's work area there was a three-and-a-half-foot-tall yellow metal box that contained the cleaning solutions for the press. Across the front door of it FLAMMA-BLE MATERIALS was painted in red. Henry hooked a leg across the front of the box, blocking out the letters, and humped the side of it.

On the right side of Henry stood Leroy, smiling and smoking a cigarette. He dropped it still burning near Henry's feet. Leroy then brought a hand up in a closed fist in front of his mouth like he was holding a microphone, but his tongue moved around on the inside of his cheeks, bulging them out and making it look like he sucked and moved his tongue all around and over something big in his mouth.

Zero kept a blank stare over the woman's shoulder.

"You haven't been working here long enough for a paid vacation. You won't get one for a while still," said Sarah. A look of annoyance was growing on her face. Her glasses slipped down her nose, and she pushed them back up.

Before he met Sarah, Zero had not been aware that women who wore glasses turned him on. When he looked back on his life though, he could see how this had always been true. "We talked about this last week," said Zero. "My vacation's in six weeks, but I wanted my pay in advance because I'm looking for a new place to live." This was not true, but Zero did not trust Sarah to pay him.

Over her shoulder, Leroy and Henry were still at it. The two of them now stood side by side with their legs bent slightly at the knees, backs bent and legs bowed open wide in an oval shape. They thrust their crotches forward and made a motion with a closed fist moving from their crotches out forward, then back again, over and over. They alternated the hand going upward in an arc to their own mouths, then back to their crotches.

"What time are you supposed to be here in the morning?" asked Sarah, irritated as Zero gazed over her shoulder.

"Nine-thirty," said Zero. He scratched at the side of his nose.

"What's the matter with your nose?" demanded Sarah, suspiciously.

"Nothing's the matter with my nose," said Zero.

"Who told you to come at 9:30?"

"You did."

"Since when?"

"Since always."

"You know you're lucky you have a job," said Sarah, smiling.

"I checked the union contract," said Zero.

Sarah turned red in the face, opening her eyes wide and flaring her nostrils. "You are not in the union!" She cut off the words, thick with contempt.

"You paid me one week last year. This year I get two. Or whatever percentage for the number of hours I work a week." Zero saw Henry and Leroy were down on their hands and knees now, pretending they were dogs. Henry sniffed at Leroy's ass, then proceeded to mount him.

"I can do whatever I want," said Sarah. "You're not protected by the union." She stood there searching for other words. "Get out of my office!" she screamed.

Zero smiled, looking all around him at the warehouse.

"Get back to work then!" screamed Sarah. She turned to walk away, then stopped. "I don't want to see anymore of that writing on the wall in the bathroom. It's not cute, whichever one of you clowns is doing it. I want it to stop. And don't hang around the shop after your shift is over anymore. I want you to go home."

Zero stood there for a moment while the woman walked off. He was exhausted by the conversation. He saw Henry and Leroy were back at their jobs when she passed by them. Leroy scooped huge armfuls of paper and put them in a bin for recycling; Henry stooped over and pushed a two-foot stack of freshly printed stationery on a small cart with wheels over toward the wall. They kept at it until the woman left the room.

Leroy soon came over to where Zero was standing, taking inventory of the new shipments of paper that had come in the day before. Zero held a clipboard and checked off what he found.

"You gotta smoke for me?" Leroy asked Zero. He was a green-eyed black man who always needed a shave.

"That's three you owe me," said Zero, handing one over. "I'm keeping count."

"Match?" Leroy grinned a mouth full of rotten teeth, taking the matches handed to him and lighting his cigarette. "I saw the dollar man at the Square there yesterday," he said. He blew the smoke out in a large cloud above both their heads. "He's gonna be there today too, he said."

Sometimes Leroy offered to get Zero some Codeine Number 3s. Zero didn't much like codeine or buying them from Leroy, though he had before. He could never be sure where Leroy had got them from. When Leroy had his neck

```
         Checked out item summary for
            JOHNSON YVONNE MANHOO
             12-02-2008 2:23PM

BARCODE: R0113203913
LOCATION: istkx
TITLE: The secret of Shadow Ranch / by C
DUE DATE: 12-13-2008

BARCODE: 33477454456244
LOCATION: iyacv
TITLE: Chance Fortune and the Outlaws /
DUE DATE: 12-13-2008

BARCODE: 33477457639930
LOCATION: infcw
TITLE: Lost at school : why our behavior
DUE DATE: 12-15-2008

BARCODE: 33477004789693
LOCATION: hloow
TITLE: Three complete novels / Dean R. K
DUE DATE: 01-02-2009

BARCODE: R0104395046
LOCATION: istkw
TITLE: Calle 10 : a novel / by Danny Rom
DUE DATE: 12-30-2008  **IN USE BY SYSTEM

BARCODE: 33477000731672
LOCATION: iaccw
TITLE: Forever Odd / by Dean Koontz.
DUE DATE: 01-13-2009  * RENEWED
```

slashed by his girlfriend and came back to work with a prescription, Zero was able to buy some for a dollar each, knowing Leroy liked a bottle of Wild Irish Rose wine better than any narcotic. Now on the rare occasion that Zero gave Leroy money, Leroy never came back with all the pills, claiming he had bought them from someone who over-charged.

Once Leroy had given Zero some capsules as payment on a debt, though he could not tell Zero what they were. "I know you're gonna like them," he had said, putting them in Zero's hand. "Now I don't owe you nothing," Leroy had said, grin-ning.

"Fuck you, you don't owe me nothing," Zero said. "What are these?"

"Put 'em away. Put 'em away. Here comes that fine bitch Sarah," said Leroy.

Zero put the handful of capsules in his shirt pocket. Sarah glanced over at the two of them but did not come over.

"I don't remember what they are," said Leroy, moving away. "I gotta get going. My old lady gets out of jail tonight, and I'm gonna do me some fucking." He stood for a moment, moving his hips back and forth, humping the air and cack-ling. "I wouldn't give you nothing that was no good," said Leroy, walking off.

"Eh, you still owe me. Don't forget," Zero had called after him.

For a few days he carried the capsules around with him, though he did not take them. When he finally threw them in the toilet he saved one and slipped it into his mouth, like a fool, he later learned. All that entire evening he had been ill.

Today Leroy was insistent. "I know the dollar man is gonna be there. Give me some money and I'll get you some." Leroy made small sweeps with his broom, trying to look busy. "I'm getting an advance on my pay tomorrow. Loan me five till then," said Leroy, giving up.

"Fuck you," said Zero, unbelieving.

Leroy acted like he was angry. "What you say?"

"Fuck you," said Zero, tired of Leroy today. He dropped the clipboard and moved closer to him.

"Dollar man is gonna be there, I know," said Leroy, moving away and continuing his sweeping across the warehouse floor.

In the afternoon Zero spent his time going through the boxes of files he maintained as part of his job. There were three different sizes because of the three different size printing presses. The largest files were kept in the warehouse. The two smaller sizes were kept up on shelves in a room behind the warehouse and the front office. The shelves were metal structures, eight-feet tall and attached to the wall. When he first started working at Company Printing, the files of old print jobs had been all in disarray due to a succession of incompetent employees that preceded Zero. It had been a dull and dusty job getting them back in order, but Zero had done it enthusiastically, grateful at the time to have found a job.

The files contained all that was needed to easily reprint a

previous job: plates, negatives, samples, and specifications, all included in an envelope. Zero had to use a ladder in order to see the files on the top shelf. Up there he had learned he could hide away from the frenzy of the print shop.

Business had been slow lately, which is why Zero was looking through these old files, making sure they contained all that they were supposed to and were still in order. He wanted to keep busy because Sarah was watching him. She was the one not bringing in new work, thought Zero, but he would be the one to be let go. Sometimes within the old files Zero found things of interest: flyers and posters for concerts and festivals, or a catalog of dildos and lesbian leather fashion.

These days Zero didn't even mind doing the UPS if O'Reilly, who usually did it, was out on delivery. They could not trust Leroy to do it correctly. Zero was glad to have something to do, as long as the boxes weren't too heavy or there weren't too many of them. Or as long as he had nothing else to do that was more fun, like typing.

Now as he stood above the rest of the company, hidden within the farthest corner of the files, Zero yawned and day-dreamed. No one had come looking for him for more than thirty minutes. The phone was being answered by Sarah or Marilyn upstairs. He sat down for a moment on the top step of the ladder. His stomach growled, and he thought he would call La Wilma later and ask if she wanted to eat Chinese food that night. There was a small hole-in-the-wall restaurant near her work that Zero didn't even mind leaving a tip at, since the food was so good and reasonably priced, though the service was lousy.

He was startled by the phone ringing and waited to see if it would be answered by anyone. He was beginning to step down when the phone was picked up. He stood again on the top step and noticed that above the files he could see straight into the front office through a gap where two walls did not meet properly.

Sarah stood alone in the room, skimming through the pages of a magazine. She leaned over the front counter, her shapely ass sticking, invitingly, up into the air. She pushed her glasses up on her nose and stuck a finger up there for a moment, digging. She then raised her left leg up onto the counter, stretching.

At one time in her life she claimed to have danced ballet, but none of the men cared if it were true or not, except they liked to watch her raise her legs. The woman looked around the room for a moment, then thinking she was by herself she stood and put a hand down the front of her pants, rubbing. Zero grew hard watching. Sarah then went back to the counter, raising a leg up on top of it again, and rubbed herself against the wooden edge. She half lay on the counter top, undulating. Her left hand reached back, cupping an ass cheek and digging with an ever-increasing fervor into the crack of her ass, searching, probing. Just then a customer walked in through the front door.

At Calle 10 Henry came into the sala with a stereo receiver underneath one arm and a tape deck under the other. He was excited and sweating, bouncing around on his tiptoes for a second and trying to catch his breath. He put the equipment down on the table in the middle of the room.

Zero had been standing at the telephone, listening to it ring over and over at La Wilma's without an answer. He wondered what she was up to, then hung the phone up, embarrassed when Henry walked in.

"What's happening?" asked Zero.

Henry caught his breath and began a little dance, singing and shuffling around the floor. "Vamos a bailar. Chicano. Vamos a chingar. Chicano." He weaved his way around the chairs surrounding the table. "Vamos a bailar. Chicano." Then Henry danced his way back out of the room.

Zero went over and checked out the stereo. Both pieces looked brand-new to him.

A minute later Henry came bursting back into the room, this time with his arms full with two huge speakers. They were held pushed together in front of his chest. Henry turned sideways to get through the doorway.

"What's going on?" asked Zero.

Henry bent his knees and lowered his body first, then the speakers, to the floor, one by one. "Eh, bro'," said Henry, as if he had just noticed for the first time that Zero was in the room. Henry took a bundle of speaker wire out of his sweat-jacket pocket and tried to strip one end of it with his teeth. He gnawed on the wire.

"What's happening with you?" Zero swept his hand over the stereo on the table and the speakers on the floor.

"Not much, bro'," said Henry, nonchalantly. He spit out a bit of plastic.

"Where'd you get all this?" asked Zero.

"What's that, bro'?"

"This stereo," said Zero. "Right here." He reached out to touch the receiver to emphasize his point, but decided against it. He didn't want his fingerprints on it, in case it was stolen.

"Oh, bro'," said Henry, surprisedly. "That's right, I got a stereo." He put down the speaker wire and took some power cords out of his other jacket pocket. "I didn't know what you was talkin' 'bout, bro'. Yeah, I got a stereo."

"You get a good deal?" Zero took a chair out from the table and sat. "Where you going to put it?"

"Oh yeah," said Henry. He chuckled. "A real good deal, ese." Henry fiddled behind the tape deck, connecting the cords. "Eh, this is going to be right here for everybody to use," he said. "I want this to be your happy home, too, ese. Look in that drawer by the phone, bro', and see if there's some pliers in there, ese."

Zero opened the drawer and pushed the papers around inside. "Eh, I don't think there are any in here. It just looks like paper and pens and shit. What's this?" Zero held up a black film canister. He shook it, then opened it. There was a small amount of grass inside.

"Let me jus' get this thing hooked up here, bro', and then we'll be jamming, ese…. You find those pliers in there?" Henry was now down on his knees underneath the table fumbling with some tangled cords and wires near the electrical outlet. "I got me a real good deal, ese. Ha, ha, ha, bro'."

"I found some weed," said Zero.

Henry turned around to see. "Nah, man, that thing's been empty a long-ass time, bro'."

"There's a little bit left," said Zero. "Check it out." He tossed it across the room.

Henry picked the canister up from off the floor. "Right on, bro'," said Henry, looking inside. "I been on the wagon for a couple of days now. I don't know how you do it. You wanna roll it up?" Henry put the canister down on top of the table and went back to his work underneath. "You didn't find no pliers, did you, bro'?"

"I'm going to go eat first," said Zero. "I didn't find nothing but the weed." He stood and headed toward the kitchen but stopped short of going inside. "Eh, Henry," he said, "we got a mouse crawling across the counter here."

"Don't worry 'bout it, bro'," said Henry from under the table. "You're bigger than it."

Zero still hesitated in the doorway.

"You can go in, bro'," said Henry. He was standing right behind Zero. "What's up, bro'?"

"Check it out," said Zero. He pointed to the counter—which was crowded with empty beer cans, used paper plates, empty frozen food boxes, and crumbs—to a spot by an empty brown grocery bag.

"I don't see nothing, bro'," said Henry. He was now standing near the overflowing garbage bag on the other side of the counter, opposite Zero. There was a thirty-pound bag of dry dog food there. It was waist high and wide open. Henry's feet were in a small pile of the meaty chunks. He reached over and moved the grocery bag. The mouse went running toward Zero.

"Get it, bro'," said Henry.

Zero moved closer, not knowing how he was supposed to stop the creature. All he could think of doing was smashing it. He grabbed a skillet from the stove.

It was a good-sized mouse, three inches long, not including the tail. It stopped and turned back around toward Henry.

"Get it, Henry," said Zero.

The mouse made its way swiftly over the plates and around the beer cans, then down the side and into the cabinet below through a door left slightly ajar.

Henry closed the cabinet door and, grabbing a broom from nearby, propped it up against it. "We'll see if it starves," he said, then walked across the room.

"Damn, I'm hungry now," said Henry. He opened the refrigerator, looking inside. "I'm gonna have me a sandwich. How 'bout you, bro'?" He started pulling things out and crowding them onto the counter. All lined up were a head of iceberg lettuce, a tomato, a loaf of bread, and a package of lunch meat. The package had not been closed properly and a slice of what looked like salami was folded underneath it.

Zero put the skillet down and watched. "I'm going over to eat at el taco truck," he said.

"Is that the one in the parking lot of the Jalisco Bar?" asked Henry. He unscrewed the top off a jar of mayonnaise and scooped a large gob of it onto a knife, some of it trailing down to the floor. "Fuck, it got on my shoe," said Henry. He put the knife and jar down on the counter. "Look at this shit," he said. He found a piece of paper and bent over and wiped his shoe.

"Yeah, on Calle 19 and the Boulevard," said Zero. "They have good comida."

Henry sliced tomato on the counter. "You want me to make you a sandwich, ese?"

"Nah, that's all right," said Zero.

Henry continued, "Eh, you see that barmaid I like, tell her I want some chi-chis." He ripped leaves from the head of lettuce and placed them on slices of bread.

"Eh, Henry," said Zero, "don't you think you should wipe off the counter before you put your food down on it like that?"

"Oh yeah, you're right, bro'." Henry tossed a couple of beer cans down to the floor and stacked up some of the plates. "Eh, here's the pliers, ese," he said. On top of the refrigerator he found a towel, then he lifted the slices of bread, one by one, and wiped underneath. He then did the same with the lettuce, tomato, and lunch meat.

"I'll be back in a little while," said Zero, walking out of the room.

Henry called after him, "Eh, watch out for those crazy motherfuckers out there, bro'."

These nights at Calle 10 Zero was all alone. He realized this was one of the reasons he had stayed living there so long. Because they lived so far away from each other, La Wilma and Zero did not spend many weeknights together. It was a long bus ride from her door to his. And it was an agreement they never made verbal that brought them together on weekends.

Some Friday and Saturday nights, La Wilma would catch Zero nodded out in front of the television, the picture already gone fuzzy. "Go home, ese," she would say, "if you don't want to fall asleep with me. And give me a couple of dollars for electricity. You're always using it when you're here, ese."

"You got it all wrong," said Zero. But she didn't seem to think so. And Zero knew if she ever found out about the H and all the rest it would be over.

On good days Zero would think of his space at Calle 10 as his own little hole-in-the-ground, secure and shielded from the outside world. It was a mess, that was true, but his room was his own squalor. And at least there was no dog food in Zero's room.

When no one else was around Zero would sit in the sala and watch the television or listen to the stereo while he ate his burrito or tacos from el taco truck for dinner. Every time he ate there he could not believe how good the food tasted. And the prices! Two dollars for a burrito or torta; one dollar for a taco! And the choices: de asada, de cabeza, de carnitas, de cessos y lengua! During the forty days of Lent Zero ordered, "sin carne," beans and rice only. And the condiments:

Radishes! Jalapeños! Cebolla! Guacamole! Chile! How lucky and proud it made him feel to be Mexican.

He stopped cooking in the kitchen shortly after he moved in. Henry never cleaned it like he said he would, and no one else felt it was his job to do so.

Henry sometimes said to Zero, "Eh, ese, we never had no mouses in the house before you moved in, ese."

Zero ignored him and restricted his kitchen use to occasional cans of sardines in Tabasco sauce. He would buy a couple rolls from the grocery store down the street and ask for a plastic fork and knife also. He ate in his room when there were others around. He did not like to eat in front of them while they ate what they had cooked in the kitchen or in the grime of the outside BBQ pit.

Six men lived in the house. There were three rooms on the ground floor and three on the second. Tyrone lived up on the top floor. He was a security guard and often worked a double shift at the Giant Supermarket. If he was not at work he was asleep in his room or smacked out or both.

Next to him lived Carl. Carl was a quiet, middle-aged black man from Louisiana who worked as a janitor and was a drunk. Tyrone always complained that Carl owed him twenty-five dollars from a long-ass time ago, when he loaned him the money for his rent to move in. But Carl said he didn't remember anything of the sort. He always maintained he was still living in the South at the time Tyrone alleged the loan took place. As Tyrone explained it to Zero, Zero found himself not believing the story.

Tyrone said, "He be sneaking in and out of this motherfuckin' place 'cause he better not let me catch his black ass and he know it."

At the other end of the hall from Tyrone lived Alexander. Tyrone told Zero he thought Alexander was queer, and he always made fun of his punk-rock friends.

"I oughta ask that little white boy for a blowjob one day," said Tyrone. "He ain't never here 'cause the faggot is always out for that dick. The best dick-sucking I ever got was from these faggots. They'd be sucking my dick good all day long back en Nuevamotherfuckin' York. And we be shooting up motherfuckin' dope all the time. Me and my partner Jimmy didn't care if they was faggots. They always gave us dope and sucked our dicks and fed us. Man, they treated us like kings. And the dick-sucking was good." Tyrone picked at his crotch.

There was a staircase that led from the backyard up to the second floor. And another that led from the second floor down to the bathroom.

Though Pancho lived in the room next door to Zero's, the only way to know for sure that Pancho was home was when he was passed out and snoring so loudly that the sound could be heard throughout the house. Also, during the summer months he sat with his door wide open, two fans running inside his room, and the stink of his sweat filled the house. It was unbearable. As was the smell of cat shit that sometimes came from the room, though Zero had never once heard a cat meow inside there. When Pancho was a kid, he and his family had been migrant farm workers all over the state and in Washington and Texas.

If Henry came into the sala while Zero sat eating and watching television or listening to the stereo, Henry would switch the channel or station without asking. Zero was not sure if he meant to be rude.

Most of the time, though, Henry was not around. Zero wondered where he was at sometimes, not because he really cared, but every night people came over at all hours looking for Henry, often two or three separate callers. When Henry did leave a message for someone about where he was going, it was more often than not the wrong information. Henry always said he was going down to his ex's house, though he claimed to have more than one.

When the ex-wife Zero knew about did call, right away she was pissed at Zero in place of Henry. She accused Zero of covering up for Henry, which Zero did every chance he was given in regard to this woman, but never on the occasions she accused him of.

Zero would say, "Eh, I don't know. He just went out not too long ago. He didn't say where he was going. Would you like to leave a message?"

Henry's ex was furious at Zero's cordiality. "I know that bastard is there, motherfucker. You little shit! Put him on the phone, goddamn it, before you die. Cocksucker!"

"Eh, fuck you," said Zero. "He's not here." He hung up the phone. The encounter frightened him.

When he next saw Henry, Zero told him what had happened. Henry grimaced in pain as the story unfolded.

"That bitch," said Henry. He turned his eyes up in a look of disgust. "That's what she said, huh? Tell me, bro'. Those are the exacted words she used? We need to document this, bro'." Henry rummaged through the drawer in the telephone table, pulling out a pencil and piece of paper. "Tell me exactedly what she said, bro'. The exacted words. Now that was cocksucker, right, bro'?" Henry licked the point of the pencil before writing.

Every night people came looking for Henry. They would stomp up the steps and across the porch, then bang on the aluminum screen door. They would then cough or clear their throats.

Zero would shout, "Who is it?" through the closed door. There was no peephole in the door or a window in the entrada through which the porch could be seen. In Henry's room there was a window, but the view was bad, and Zero did not want to go in there anyway.

Sometimes they would not answer Zero but just walk off. Other times it would be two or three in the morning and a group of them would be laughing loudly and smashing cans and clinking together bottles of booze as they came over to party with Henry.

One of the group on the porch would shout back, "Yeah, homeboy, is Henry in there? He told us to come by here to meet him, ese."

But Zero never let them in, and when Henry finally showed up three days later, he was drunk and had forgotten his house key and came tapping on Zero's window about 5 AM. Zero told him about the group that came looking for him and gave him their names.

Henry bugged his eyes out, looking scared. "Eh, I never heard of those people, ese," said Henry. "I wonder how did they know where I lived anyway? I hope you didn't let those crazy motherfuckers inside the pad, ese. You never know what those crazy motherfuckers is thinking or gonna 'bout to do."

Most of the time those that came knocking at the door in the middle of the night left without a hassle. They were even apologetic and understanding. "Hey, we're sorry. We didn't mean to wake you up," they would say. "You wanna beer? You don't have to open the door. We'll just leave it out here on the porch and you can get it when we leave or tomorrow or whenever, ese."

Zero opened the door only when Ray came over, and this grew to be more and more often. Ray was a married man, but he stayed away from his wife and three children as much as he could, it seemed, the way married men sometimes do. In the sala the two men would sit and smoke.

Ray told Zero, "Eh, I envy all you guys living here. You know that, Zero? You can do whatever you want. You're FREE!" He punched the air when he said this. "There's mostly no kids here," he went on, "And no bitches nagging. You can bring one over whenever you want and then tell her to get the hell out of your house when you want. And you can probably just ask that Alexander for a blowjob if you wanted to. I know that guy's a homo. Eh, and I can't smoke no weed at my pad like here." Ray brought out a shiny brass pipe from his pocket. Next he took out from beneath his windbreaker jacket a large freezer bag full of marijuana.

Zero opened his eyes up wide at the size of the bag, even though Ray was always bringing over this homegrown. Zero had never asked Ray where he got it from, but he knew the man could not afford to buy it. "Right on," said Zero.

Ray filled the pipe with grass. "My wife says this shit makes me crazy," he said. "They complain 'cause I have the music too loud. And I'll be sitting there in the middle of the room, tripping out on it. But I can't smoke in the pad. I sneak outside or go down the street for a drive or come here." He lit the green leaves and puffed on the smoke.

"Eh, you shouldn't be carrying it around like that," said Zero. "You better leave it here."

Ray shook his head "no" when Zero said this. He stopped puffing on the smoke and held it in, sitting there and smiling at Zero. He let it out, then smoked some more before passing it to Zero.

"You took long enough," said Zero, taking the pipe.

"I can't even keep it in the house," said Ray. "I gotta keep it in my car trunk. I just put it in my jacket when I got out front. My old lady will find it if I leave it in the pad. Or my son, Ramon. He knows things now. He's in junior high school. Sometimes I think he is looking in my eyes to see if I'm stoned when I get home from here. It's like he knows I been smoking or something."

When Zero handed Ray the pipe again, Ray knocked the ashes out on the table top, then brushed them onto the floor. He then refilled the bowl and gave it back to Zero.

"My old lady doesn't smoke," said Ray. "Nor drink. But that's all right as long as she don't stop sucking my dick. Ha, ha, ha." He took the pipe passed to him and puffed on it.

Once when the two of them had gone out to the Red Neck Bar in Barrio San Pablo, Ray said it was his birthday and asked Zero to buy him a beer. Zero wanted to see proof before he would do it. Ray complied, and Zero was surprised that Ray was telling the truth. He gladly bought him a beer.

Six months later in another bar on the other side of town, Ray said the same thing to Zero. Again Zero asked for an ID to prove it, and again Ray complied. Zero noticed this time though that the ID made Ray three years older than before. He bought him the beer anyway and didn't ask about it.

"That fat broad out in the Valley," said Ray, "she smokes yesca like a chimney. Like there's no tomorrow, I'm telling you. She usually has some good stuff, too. Bud. Not like this homegrown I always got." He passed the pipe to Zero.

"Eh, what do you have, a farm of grass or what out in the Valley?" Zero smiled, then puffed on the pipe.

Ray's face turned red. He fumbled over his words. "No, what are you talkin' 'bout? I don't got shit. You know that." Ray quickly took a cigarette from his pocket and brought it to his mouth all in one motion.

"You got a lot of weed you always bring over," said Zero. "You know what I mean?"

"Eh, what are you a narc? Or what?" said Ray. He took the

cigarette out of his mouth. "You want me to stop bringing it over then? Is that what you want? I'll do that and take my fat ass home with it. If that's what you want now?"

"Eh, man, be cool," said Zero. "What's your problem? I'm just looking to buy some, you know me. That's all. You don't have to tell me anything. I was just wondering. You're always saying how easy it would be."

Ray stood up suddenly, blurting out. "Eh, man, all right. I know where the shit is grown. All right. But that's all I'm saying. This shit ain't mine. I'm not growing it, but I can have as much as I want. That's the truth now. What are you, a narc? You better not be." He sat back down flustered at his own outburst.

Zero pushed the pipe across the table top.

Ray took it and filled it. "I think I'm gonna go see that fat broad in the Valley this weekend," he said. He handed the pipe to Zero. "I was getting a hard-on earlier, thinking about her."

"Eh, I don't give a fuck," said Zero. He put a match to the grass.

Late one night Zero walked into the sala. Henry and Ray were sitting at the table, loaded. It looked like laundry day again for Henry. Zero was sure it was the third day that week. The air in the room was dank from the garbage bags filled with wet clothes. Henry was trying to explain something to Zero. He was groggy from pain killers and malt liquor. "Eh, ... I don't know, homes. I guess you're just not around ...

when I get these good numbers.... " Henry nodded out for a minute.

Ray stood against the wall. His eyes were also glazed, his movements sluggish. "That shit was good, Zero," he said, grinning.

Henry was still talking, more to himself. "And I know you got me that H, that one time ... but I ... I ... can't be doing that shit like I want to.... " He raised a quart bottle of Colt 45 and drank from it. He splashed the front of his shirt and pants.

"He's all fucked up," said Ray. He drank from his own bottle. "He took four of them, man. He's crazy." Ray laughed.

"It's not like I'm holding out ... or anything," said Henry. "Or anything like that...." His eyes went out of focus, then his head hit his chest.

"You wouldn't believe that shit either," said Ray. "That shit was sooo gooooood! You know you really missed out this time. I hope your old lady was sucking your dick good, 'cause that shit is something else!" He asked Henry, "What was that shit, anyways?"

Henry lifted his hand, a small wave, then dropped it. He smiled stupidly, not answering. The quart bottle fell out of his lap, and he followed it to the floor.

The two went to pick him up. Henry was all dead weight. "Eh, fuck it," said Ray. "Let's leave him on the floor here. He'll be all right."

Zero said, "Let's just drag him into his room. That'll be better. Get him out of the way. Grab an arm."

"This motherfucker is out!" said Ray, laughing. The quart bottle spilled over the floor. A puddle formed around Henry. The change fell out of Henry's pants pockets as they dragged him off into the darkness, his feet scraping across the floor.

Shortly after, they were at the table again. Zero turned on the television and flipped through the channels with the remote control.

"I have to get up early tomorrow," said Ray. "I gotta take my kids and their class on a field trip. I gotta drive them in the afternoon. I better go. I gotta be there at 1 PM." He stood to leave the room, then turned quickly toward the kitchen. "Eh, what's that?" he said. Ray cocked his ear toward the other room. "Turn that down. Turn that down," he told Zero.

Zero turned the television off and froze in his place. He didn't know what Ray had just heard. Maybe it's some motherfucker trying to break in, thought Zero.

"You hear that?" asked Ray. He moved across the room, now standing in the doorway to the kitchen.

Zero shook his head "no."

Ray walked into the kitchen, turning back with a smile. "I can hear the mice now," he said. "How 'bout you?" He leaned his head over the side of the counter. "Man, you should check this out," said Ray. He hurried back into the sala.

"What's going on?" asked Zero. He sat up straight, a little anxious.

"Eh, I can hear them in there. Inside the cupboard," said Ray. "There must be a bunch of them in there. Can't you hear them?" He sat back down.

"No, I can't hear them," said Zero. He turned his head toward the kitchen. "I thought Henry said he caught the mouse."

"Yeah. One this morning. And two or three, I forget, the day before yesterday," Ray said, matter of factly.

Zero swallowed hard. His stomach suddenly felt empty, and he needed something for his parched throat. He wondered if he had a Snappy Tom in his room.

Ray went on, "I can't believe how much noise they make. Like they own the place. That would drive me crazy. They are bold!" He laughed.

"Do they sound big?" asked Zero. "I still can't hear them."

Ray leaned back in his chair. "Oh, you know, regular size." He looked around the room, then toward the floor. "Eh, look at that," he said, pointing over near the doorway where the floor met the wall. "You see that—that's mouse shit. Yeah, man, they are here and have been for a while. That's why they act so bold. Like now."

"Fucking Henry always says they had no mice before I moved in." Zero sounded angry.

"No way," said Ray. "These ones are bold. You know they have been here for a while. Probably generations. You see they don't even care if there are humans, like us, around or not. They go on and make all the noise they want. And do whatever the fuck they want. It doesn't matter who's around or not. You know what I mean?"

"Yeah. I know," said Zero.

"Eh, and you see this." Ray walked over to the doorway

and pointed into the kitchen. "You see that bag of dog food over in the corner there. They love that shit right there, man. They eat it all day long I bet and tell all their friends about it. This is probably some high-class restaurant, a Sizzler, in the mouse world. You know that? That's thirty pounds of breakfast, lunch, and dinner right there, homeboy. They love that shit. They in your room yet?"

"What do you mean, *yet?*" asked Zero.

"Let's look," said Ray, already heading on his way down the hallway to Zero's room. Zero followed him.

"Eh, what are you doing?" asked Zero, standing in the doorway of his room.

Ray was over by Zero's bed. He had pushed it away from the windows and was down on his knees, looking at the floor where it met the gray-green colored, mold-covered wall. "I'm looking for mouse shit," said Ray, sounding a little irritated at the question. "Yeah. You see all this little black shit down here is mouse shit." He stood up and brushed his knees off. "How 'bout in here?" He stepped over to the closet and opened the door.

"Eh," said Zero, "what are you doing?" He moved quickly across the room to Ray.

Ray was down on his knees in the doorway of the closet. "Yeah. You can see it all in here, too." His head was in the corner.

"Get out of there," said Zero.

"Okay, bro'," said Ray. He struggled to get to his feet. "Eh, I'd be careful when you are sleeping. You don't want those things getting all over you and crawling on your face or into your mouth. Those things are gross and carry diseases and shit like that. Man, I'd watch out if I was you."

"You really think so," said Zero. He sat down on the edge of his bed, dejected.

"Eh, I know so, bro'," said Ray. "A cousin of mine died once back en Mexico from a rat that bit him. And I don't know much about mouse shit really, but either you got a whole bunch of them mice in this house or you got a smaller number of rats." He folded his arms across his chest authoritatively, bringing his speech to an end.

Zero started throwing things into a backpack. "I think I'll go see what my old lady is doing," he said.

Ray looked surprised. "What do you mean?" he asked. "It's already three in the morning. Won't she get mad?" He smiled his big white teeth.

"Yeah. Well. It'll be okay," said Zero.

Ray jumped slightly in his place. "Eh, you hear that?" he asked. He stepped closer to the closet, cocking his ear toward the door. "Man, those motherfuckers are all over the place." Ray laughed.

Zero started packing his bag quicker.

"Yeah, maybe it is a good idea you don't stay here tonight. They'd probably be crawling all over your face and waking you up. You know what I mean? You don't want them to bite you," said Ray. He smiled. "And I bet those things are big ones, too. From the way I can hear them all over the place and shitting over everywhere like they own the place." He moved his head again, back out toward the hallway. He opened his eyes up wider. "Can you hear them?" he whispered.

Zero sat still for a long moment on the edge of the bed, listening intently. "No, I can't hear them," he said, swallowing hard. He glanced around the room, looking for something to drink. "But that's okay," said Zero, "because I know those motherfuckers are around. And have been around for a long time before I ever moved in. Man. The way Henry keeps this place with the dog food and garbage bags all over and piles of clothes and aluminum cans. And the fucking dog, Tangerine, that bitch. And Pancho's room smells like cat shit. And the kitchen. Sometimes I think I should move."

"When you gonna move out?" asked Ray, suddenly sounding disappointed. "I didn't know you was moving out."

"Eh, I don't know. Forget it," said Zero. His bag was packed, and he threw it over his shoulder.

"Eh, I'll give you a ride down to catch the bus. You're taking the bus?"

"Okay," answered Zero. He and Ray stepped out of the room.

The bus was crowded with the usual assortment of diseased-looking drunks, junkies, sissies, and whores and those carrying lunch pails and Thermoses on their way home from an odd-houred shift at the refinery where the bus route began. The transit station trains stopped running at midnight, and in general Zero rode the bus because it was less expensive. The #72 was one of the few remaining bus lines that still ran all night and connected the two counties, covering a distance of more than thirty miles of city.

Zero did not know where he was going. There was no way he could go to La Wilma's at this hour. In another lifetime, it seemed to Zero now, he would have wakened her, screwed her, then borrowed money before leaving to drink again with his friends waiting outside in the car. How long ago that seemed at times, and at others he remembered it with shame like it was yesterday. If he phoned her now she would only hang up on him. He knew that for certain. In two or three hours he could call her and go over. She would be awake by then and getting ready for work.

There was no traffic, and the bus sped down the street. In the morning when he went to work it took Zero an hour at least. The same in the evening when he rode it home. He usually read the newspaper or a novel. If he made the mistake of catching the bus in the middle of a weekday, it was a sweaty, jam-packed ride that took nearly two hours. Right now it would be only thirty minutes, or less. When he got to downtown Oakland, he figured, he would go to an all-night diner and have some breakfast and coffee.

He took a postcard out of his backpack and addressed it to his family en El Sur. The picture on the card was of the Boulevard in Ciudad Jimenez, looking east from Calle 19. It was a world of thirty years ago and showed the sidewalks bustling with pedestrians shopping on a Saturday afternoon, the street filled with auto traffic and the city thriving and prospering—all fueled by the refinery. A giant refinery billboard towered over the entire scene. It was nothing like the ghost town it was today. Zero wrote on the postcard:

Gente,

> *Things are well en Ciudad Jimenez. How are you all? You should come to El Norte some day to visit. I got my shotgun. No stock. No barrel. No problem. Ha, ha, ha.*

> *LOVE,*
> *El Zero*

He put a stamp on the card and put it away in the backpack to mail later. In the distance he could see the Tribune Tower building through the front windshield of the bus. He prepared to get off soon.

At 12th Street Zero stepped off, across from the Tribune Tower. There was a diner, he thought he remembered, nearby. He could picture it vaguely: mostly pitchers of beer and a jukebox. He looked up at the clock atop the tower and saw that it was nearly four in the morning. He still had at least two hours before he could call La Wilma and go over.

It took him some time to find the diner, walking east on 12th Street for about a half mile before turning back. The streets were deserted, except for a few crackheads. Zero was glad he had brought his gray jacket with the metal bar he kept in the pocket. Then he started worrying the police would roust him and find the weapon and was glad when he got back to the Tribune Tower and someone told him the diner was on 11th Street, behind the Tower building. Zero headed that way, feeling like an idiot.

Inside the diner he remembered the surroundings more like something that had been described to him than a place he had actually been to before. Then he remembered they had thrown him out of here once or twice. The last time was when he had just been released from a night in the jailhouse nearby, and he stopped here and drank until all his money was gone and still wanted more beer on credit. All the night before that, while locked up, he kept telling everyone inside he was going to get drunk as soon as he got out and that was the reason he had been pulled off the streets in the first place. The arresting officers themselves heard him saying this over and over and kept him in there longer than usual because of his big mouth.

Zero noticed immediately when he walked in the pretty Mexican waitress working there. He could not be sure if she had been there when he was thrown out, but he did not feel uncomfortable speaking to her. He ordered coffee, scrambled eggs, bacon, and toast. Then when the waitress left, Zero looked in his pocket for some money.

Another time he had been in here after looking for a job as an office clerk or proofreader, he couldn't remember which for certain, at the *Tribune* newspaper. He had got all dressed up with a sports coat, some faded jeans, and a pin-striped dress shirt, which he thought he looked real sharp in. But when he got to the lobby of the tower, a security guard asked him what he wanted and where did he think he was going?

Zero, surprised by the questions, answered that he was there to apply for a job. And the guard then reached into a drawer there at his own desk and pulled an application from a tablet of them and handed it to Zero. Zero never bothered filling it out and left for the diner, where he ordered a pitcher of beer and ended six days of sobriety that he had cried, prayed, and sweated to get through without drinking. The rest of the week turned into an alcoholic blur.

Outside the window near where he sat, Zero could see the bundles of the *Tribune* newspaper being loaded onto step-vans. A steady line of the vans waited, were loaded, then drove off to different parts of the county.

After a high school course in journalism, Zero thought he would someday be a reporter when he got older. His instructor was a Mr. Sanchez, a sloppily dressed Chicano from East Los Angeles, who looked more like an ex-gang member than a teacher and often appeared stoned in the morning before class and after lunch. The school was too poor to have a real newspaper, more than a few blurry mimeographed pages that were assembled and handed out once or twice a semester. Mr. Sanchez praised Zero's essays, which were usually about drug experiences and did nothing but get Zero in trouble. Mr. Sanchez was eventually fired himself, midway through the semester, according to the rumors, after an arrest for possession.

In Zero's first year in college, he was still young and ambitious and tried to get into an upper-division newswriting course. Both times he signed up he was put first on the waiting list, but no one ever dropped out and he couldn't take the course. And not long after, he found a girlfriend and spent most of his time drinking and fucking.

Outside, the loading of newspapers continued. It looked like fun, especially working at night. Zero had once worked a part-time evening shift, 5–10 PM, and enjoyed it, but never an overnight shift. He remembered his father had been on rotating shifts that last job he had before he went on disability.

It might not be so bad either, driving or loading the vans, thought Zero as he watched. It couldn't be any worse than now at Company Printing. And the Tribune probably paid better. The bosses at Company Printing, especially Sarah, were always trying to get an employee to do work even after they had clocked out for the day. Even the union workers, like Henry, were getting cheated according to the union contract, which Henry had asked Zero to read once and explain to him.

For months already Zero had practiced the speech with which he would set Sarah straight one day. He knew it would also be his last day of employment at Company Printing. First chance he got enough courage, he thought, he would do it.

As a young boy he had searched for an identity on the walls of El Sur with a spray-paint can, crayon, and felt-tip marker. He possessed little artistic ability, which did not help matters and made everything he wrote look scribbled, though sometimes more elaborately scribbled than others.

He lost God when his father died. Or whatever little bit of God he had up until then, he figured. As a boy he had always marveled at his father's own faith. The two of them were regulars at 6:30 Mass on Sunday mornings where his father was an usher. Zero remembered sitting in the church alone while his father's deep voice came from the back pew, booming over all the others' throughout the cavernous Iglesia San Luis.

Several weekends out of the year his father went away for a retreat with the Holy Name Society up to the Mountain City of the Lord Seminary. He always brought back a group photo of the men. The photos were collages of old and wrinkled, mellow and contemplative, bewildered and stern brown faces, white faces, and every year a black face or two among the rest. Family men, they all were, one could have easily guessed, thought Zero.

And as a boy, Zero remembered, he would sometimes take out the box of those group pictures just to look at his father, year after year, growing more and more gray and wrinkled, in one photo with a bushy white beard like Colonel Sanders and, in another, sleek-looking with neatly trimmed moustache and hair, the furrow deepening in his brow and his eyes always deep-set and serious-looking, like the loud, booming voice from the back of the church or coming from across the yard, through the air, from the house next door where the man spent most of his time outside of work, drinking with his best friend, Gonzalo Zamora, and his ex-convict, heroin-addict wife, Dolly.

After his meal Zero stood and walked across the room to

the cash register. He smiled at the same pretty waitress. She smiled back, then said, "You don't remember me, do you?"

Zero was perplexed. What a night it had been already, he thought. "No, I'm sorry," he said. "I don't."

The woman took a napkin and wrote on it. "Here," she said, "is my phone number. Give me a call." She gave Zero a devilish smile that truly frightened him.

"Yeah. Okay," said Zero, taking the napkin and wondering what it was all about. "Can I have a lottery ticket?" he asked, not knowing what else to say, but not wanting the conversation to end. She handed him the ticket with his change. Zero put it all in the pocket with the metal bar. He then walked out into the growing sunlight.

PART IV

That next night Zero was on the phone with his friend Joe, long distance. "You know what I'm saying," said Zero with an affected bravado. "Fuck those pigs anyway. I'll do whatever I damn well please." He held the receiver with his chin against his shoulder and took a toke of yesca from a pipe. He blew the smoke out in a cloud toward the ceiling. "So fuck their jay-walking ticket," he went on. "They can stick it in their ass." He took another toke on the pipe.

"You're not gonna pay them," said Joe on the other end. "Salud!"

Zero could hear over the phone a beer can being opened. "Eh, fuck them," said Zero, letting some smoke out. He sucked the rest back in, a trail of it going up a nostril. There was a knock at the front door. "Eh, wait a minute," said Zero.

Zero took the phone away from his ear and cocked his head toward the entrada and front door, beyond where the knocking came from. He didn't really want to answer the door, knowing it was probably someone looking for Henry. The knocking continued.

"Hold on, Joe," said Zero. He lay the receiver down on the table and tiptoed over to the door. There was still knocking. Zero stood there for a moment, then shouted, "Eh, who is it?" There was no answer.

Zero got back on the telephone. "Eh, Joe, what's happening?" He picked up the remote control and turned on the television. On the screen game show contestants, pressing a buzzer to speak first, tried to answer simple questions faster than one another.

"Eh, Zero," said Joe, hurriedly, "hold on."

Zero could hear the telephone receiver at Joe's house hit the floor. He moved his earpiece away because of the loud, sharp crack sound. Then he listened further and could hear in the background, faintly, the sound of Joe throwing up. After a minute or two of this, Joe came back on the line.

"What's happening, Zero?" asked Joe.

Zero said, "I don't know. Someone knocked on the door a couple of times, but when I asked who it was, no one answered."

Again there were the sounds of someone at the front door, feet shuffling on the porch. "Hold on," said Zero. He walked into the entrada and listened to the sounds on the other side of the door. When he put his ear against it he could hear keys jingling, then one key placed into the door lock. Zero went back to the telephone. "It must be Henry or Pancho," he said. "I guess too buzz-bombed and can't get the key in the lock." Zero laughed.

Joe laughed too. "Shit, I heard that," said Joe. "Hold on, let me get a beer."

Zero could hear over the phone the sounds of a beer can being opened.

"Yeah. All right," said Joe. "Man, Zero, I don't know. My old lady, man, she just keeps getting fatter and fatter and she don't seem to care or want to do anything about it. Man ..."

"Yeah, I hear you," said Zero. He could still hear the sounds coming from the front door. He flipped the channel on the television. Now he could see two TV cops playing by the rule book.

"What do you mean?" asked Joe.

"I don't mean anything," said Zero. "You know what I mean. I'm just agreeing with you. Go on with your story."

"Yeah, man," said Joe. "I don't know about this. She just wants to eat. That's all she fucking does. Eats. Man, you know she ain't working no more. And the kids are in school all day. And shit, I think maybe, I just want a little strange pussy. You know what I mean? Someone who's not such a fucking slob ..."

"Yeah. I hear you," said Zero. The sounds still came from the front door, but no one had come inside yet. "Hold on again, Joe," said Zero. He walked over to the door. The knob was turning, and someone was putting a shoulder against the door, trying to get it open, but the dead bolt was still on. There was the sound of keys, again, outside. Whispers, maybe, but Zero could not tell for certain.

"Eh, is that you, Henry?" Zero finally shouted.

There was silence for a second. Then there were the sounds of feet moving, abruptly off the porch they ran, then down the sidewalk, two or three pairs of them running, moving quickly, it sounded like to Zero. He opened the door to Henry's room and walked over to the window and looked outside.

He heard car doors opened and slammed shut somewhere out of his view. Then a car engine started, and the car peeled out. Zero saw the old Chevy as it squealed down the street.

The next morning Zero told Henry what he had seen.

"Bold fuckers," said Henry. "And you was sitting in here with the TV on and the lights on and everything and they still tried to come in?" he asked.

"Yeah, man," said Zero. "I asked who it was when I first heard the noise. You know how people are always coming by looking for you when you're not around."

Henry made a face like he had never heard of such a thing before in his life. "And you was the only one here? Is that right?" he asked.

"I'm the only one ever here," said Zero. "But last night no one answered me when I asked, Who is it?"

"Yeah, man," said Henry. "I been meaning to tell you where I keep my piece. But that shit with these mother-fuckers, I better let you keep something for yourself." Henry walked through the hallway to his room and beckoned Zero to follow.

Inside the dark and messy room Henry walked over to his closet and started rummaging about inside. "I gave a lot of shit away a couple of months ago," he began, "'cause I was loco with some head trips. Remember when I was out there in the backyard that one night?" Henry asked this with a smile on his face. He brought out a .22 rifle for Zero. "I gave one homeboy a shotgun," continued Henry, "and another one an Uzi. But I still got a few pieces around the pad just in case.

You never know when some pleito's gonna go down." He walked over to a dresser and looked in a top drawer. He brought out a box of bullets and filled a rifle magazine. "This holds five bullets," he said. "You better keep it loaded in your room with these bold motherfuckers 'round here." He attached the full magazine to the rifle. "To load the bullet into the chamber, you move this thing up and over. Like this." Henry showed the lever and motion to Zero without actually moving it. "Here you go," he said. He held out the gun and box of bullets.

Zero did not reach for them. "Eh, how do you take that thing with the bullets out?"

"The magazine," said Henry. "Like this. With your thumb and forefinger. You get 'em in here and squeeze and you can pull it out." He did this as he spoke, pulling the magazine out, then replacing it. "The chamber is empty," he said. "See." Henry pointed the rifle to the floor, then pulled the trigger with a flinch, a grimace on his face and his eyes closed. The rifle clicked softly. "See," he said. "You should always point it toward the ground. Never at anyone, unless you plan on blowing their fucking head off." Henry smiled.

This time when Henry held the bullets and rifle out to Zero, Zero grabbed them and carried them to his room. Henry followed.

"Eh, was they mallates?" asked Henry. "Last night."

"Chicanos," answered Zero. "Gangsters, the way they looked and their car. A real nice-looking bomb from the forties, I think. Glass packs. Ooooommmm Pppaaahhh. Mags. Real nice. I never seen it around here."

Henry swallowed hard, visibly. His eyes got shifty. "You sure 'bout that?" His voice cracked. "You sure 'bout that, ese?"

"That's what it looked like to me," said Zero.

Henry stood there, the color slowly draining out of his face.

After work Zero went straight home. Sarah warned him not to stay after he punched out, because she suspected he was smoking dope with the second shift while they still worked and drank. At Calle 10 he went to his room, then into the closet where he had put the rifle. He moved his chair over and stood on it, looking on the top shelf where the rifle lay flat, pushed back into the furthest corner. He stepped down and looked on the lowest gray metal shelf in the room for the box of bullets and fully loaded magazine. They lay partially hidden in among a stack of his credit card bills, some paper clips, pens, and a nail clipper.

Zero stepped back up on the chair and brought the rifle down. He moved the lever up and over like Henry had shown him, then pointed the barrel toward the ground. He shut his eyes and grimaced as he pulled the trigger. It went click softly. He got the magazine and attached it to the rifle, then squeezed and took it out again. He did this a couple of more times to get the hang of it. Then he did it with his eyes closed a few times. He thought, I might need to know how to load the gun real quick in the dark late one night if an intruder came into the house and I was forced to blow his fucking head off.

Zero did not have much experience with firearms. The

little that he did have was not good. When he was seventeen and growing up en El Sur, Zero was loco on smoking PCP and listening to heavy metal music. When they threw him out of high school he took to the streets and the parks during the day. Most of his friends had been expelled or had dropped out. He spent a lot of time with Roberto, the runaway, especially; the boy was lost between his divorced parents, poverty, drugs, and alcohol and could not find his way.

New Year's Eve of that year, Zero remembered the night well. He had been sitting around with Roberto. They were drinking some good brandy at Ben's house while his mother was away for the night. But what all three really wanted was some sherm, dust, superkool, the mummy: PCP.

Roberto was enthusiastic, as always, about the idea. "Man," he said, "let's fry!" He swirled the brandy around inside his can of cola, then drank from it, pursing his lips together afterwards from the harsh taste. "Whoooooo!" he said.

"Nothing's happening anywhere," said Zero. "Even my brother ain't got nothing. And can't find none."

Ben spoke up, "Why don't you go over on Hooper. You know those mallates. I saw Midget in the park during the day, and he was all fucked up on some sherm he got out there. You know those mallates, don't you?"

Later they all three walked out there in the early morning of a new year. It was unusually cold. Ben carried the bottle of liquor underneath his jacket. He was all bundled up in a nice, new thick and warm jacket, with a scarf, gloves, and sweater underneath. Zero and Roberto warmed themselves with the brandy mostly. They were both dressed in several layers of t-shirts only, underneath their worn-out light weight coats. Neither of them could afford the things Ben could, even though Zero had a weekend job cleaning out the parish hall after dances were held, and Roberto played the guilt trip on his parents so that he always had some money, though only two or three dollars at a time. And when they did have money the both of them never spent it on nice clothes or much else other than PCP, malt liquor, and metal music. Compared to his friends, Ben was rich, but not really: he was just another poor Chicano growing up in the ghetto, carrying a knife, using drugs, and drinking.

On Hooper Street they could not find anyone they knew. For close to an hour they walked all over the south of the city, through court yard after court yard filled with thugs and cra- zies, looking for Rock-Baby. Country, a tall black man in his early twenties who used to be a basketball star at some time in his short life, but who now spent his days in the park drinking Olde English 800 Malt Liquor by the quart bottle, introduced Rock-Baby to Zero and Roberto because Country knew they liked the sherm. Rock-Baby gave them the usual talk about having the best in all the ghetto, and the pair took a chance with him and had not been disappointed. But so far this year there was no sherm to be found.

Ben was drunk and vandalizing everything he could. He kept uprooting young trees and breaking off their branches. Next he would pull the five-foot-long stakes used to support the trees out of the ground, like he was Hercules. Every bottle he came across he smashed in the middle of the street.

Roberto said to him, "Eh, why don't you cut that shit out, you asshole! You want the sheriffs coming by? Dickhead!"

"Fuck you. Suck my dick." said Ben. "You're just fuckin' scared. Fuck you. Fuck the sheriffs!"

"Fuck you both," said Zero. "Be quiet. Check this out."

Down the street they saw a tall, thin cholo staggering over toward them. He looked a couple of years younger than the three of them and wore a beanie low on his head, almost covering his eyes. Otherwise he was dressed in the usual gang fashion: khakis, Pendleton, and shiny calcos. He came closer to where the three of them stood, near a street light.

Roberto said to him, "Eh, ese, you know where to score some superkool, ese?"

The young cholo stopped and turned toward them. He smelled like liquor. "You need some polvo, ese. I can get it for you. The best, ese. Let me have your money. I'll be right back. How much you want, ese?"

Zero did not like the idea. "Where do you gotta go to get it?" he asked.

"Just up the street. To my homeboy's house. I'll be right back."

Zero spoke with his two friends. "What do you think?" he asked.

"Come on," said Ben. "Let's get it."

"Yeah," said Roberto. "Let's fry!"

Zero shrugged his shoulders.

Roberto handed over a ten-dollar bill. "Where you gonna go?" asked Roberto.

"Just up the street," repeated the cholo, now pointing. "It'll take me 'bout five minutes. Be right back." He took the money and swaggered off with it.

Roberto went across the street and followed him for a little while from the other side, to see where he was going.

"He's not coming back," said Zero.

"He better," said Ben. "He's got our money."

Roberto walked back and said, "He went into the house by the parking lot, near where the preschool shit is."

Later they searched the parking lot and preschool yard, but the young cholo was nowhere to be found. Then, against any common sense, they gathered beer bottles from up and down the street and stood across from the house Roberto said he saw the thief walk into with their money—where he was probably, as they all stood there now, still laughing his head off with all his homeboys about the assholes he had just ripped off waiting down the street.

With nearly thirty bottles collected, Zero started throwing them first. He began with a six-pack, still in the carton, that went sailing through a six-foot-long picture window. The others followed in a brief rain of bottles crashing through the glass on the front door, bouncing off the car in the driveway, and gouging the wood frame of the house. Glass splintered everywhere.

Weeks later they were all three walking their usual route to their friend Julio's house. In the backyard, while his mother was away, the four would smoke and shoot dice or play odd and even for the coins in their pockets. The trio walked west on 76th Street until it dead-ended into F. D. R. Park. They crossed through, careful of the Park Patrol: armed county officers who patrolled the park and were supposed to stay within its confines, but never did, bringing their own brand of law enforcement to wherever they saw fit. Once through the park they crossed Graham Avenue to the railroad tracks.

There was a fenced-in pedestrian bridge that rose up fifty feet above the railroad tracks, so a person could cross over to where 76th Street continued. They sometimes hid up on the bridge and got high when Julio wasn't home or his mother was and they had no place else to go. Ben had brought along some cutters because they were going to cut through the fence, which had, for the first time in years, been repaired.

Ben said, "I've never seen this fucking fence fixed before. Fuck them. I've been walking through here for years."

The three of them stood on the rocks in the darkness of the railroad tracks, which were littered with broken bits of civilization. On both sides of where they stood were large factories. On the right was Wilson Drum Company. In the yard was a sight: thousands of empty fifty-five-gallon steel drums, stacked up on their sides, in piles twenty and thirty feet high, like so many rolls of pennies.

Through the fence 76th Street continued for a short distance. There were a few houses on one side of the street; on the other was the corrugated-steel wall of the drum company. One of the yards had three giant Dobermans they all had to be careful of if the gate was open. The street dead-ended again, but there was a narrow passageway that cut between Maie and Miramonte Streets. On both sides of the sidewalk was a ten-foot cyclone fence, separating the group as they walked through from the backyards of houses and the parking lot of a Baptist Church. Seventy-sixth Street continued on westward, uninterrupted, once it passed Miramonte.

Midway through the passageway they passed two cholos. Roberto stopped. "Is that the guy?" he asked the others. They all conferred for a quick moment and then hurried to catch up with the pair.

"Eh, man, hold on!" shouted Zero.

The pair halted and turned toward them. "What do you want, ese?" said the tall, thin cholo.

They all knew immediately it was the same cholo from New Year's Eve. His beanie was pulled down in the same fashion, almost covering his eyes, and the slight accent and stature were clearly recognizable.

"You owe us money," Roberto blurted out. Ben moved in closer to the group.

The second cholo spoke up, "What are these guys talkin' 'bout, ese?"

"I don't know, ese. I never seen them."

"Fuck you," said Ben.

"You stole our money," said Zero. "That's all we want."

"Fuck you, ese!" said the thief. "Don't mess with us. We're from Big Barrio Grande, ese."

Zero said to the friend, "This guy stole our money."

"Fuck, he don't got your money, ese," said the friend. "Vamonos! ese."

"Fuck you, ese!" said the tall beanie. "Don't fuck with Big Barrio Grande!"

The three of them were silent, standing still, not backing down, but knowing what that meant. They lived in that barrio: with one of the biggest and oldest gangs in the city. A person did not want to be on their bad side. Ben, among the three of them, was the only one still in high school. They liked drugs and drinking, but none of them had ever claimed gang membership, with the trouble and protection such a thing could afford a person. They let the pair walk away. Then a minute later, without saying a word to each other, they began chasing them.

The older of the two cholos threw bottles to try and slow them, but they kept on going. None of them knew what might happen if they caught up with them, but they kept running. They never knew what awaited them around the next alleyway or street corner up ahead. They chased them all the way to Middle Avenue. The pair continued farther, north up Converse Street.

The three ran back the way they had come and continued on their way to Julio's house. They ran into Jesse, who lived near the park, and told him what had just happened. "Eh, man, I don't want nothing to do with that shit," he said and split in a hurry, leaving them still standing there.

When they got to Julio's, they found he wasn't home. They went into the backyard anyway, for a minute, to rest. In near silence they shared a joint.

"Fuck those guys," said Ben.

"Yeah. Fuck them."

"Yeah. Fuck them."

They walked back up Miramonte to the passageway. Halfway through it they slowed down. All three saw the '69 Riviera drive slowly by, then speed away. They stopped in their tracks.

Then, moving more cautiously, the three continued on through to Maie, then down the short bit of 76th Street. As they approached the hole they had cut in the fence earlier, the Riviera could be seen approaching from the other side of the tracks. It came from the south, still moving slowly up Graham Avenue. All at once they saw the rifle barrel sticking out the back window. Then there were quick bursts of fire.

Another day Zero stood at the toilet at Calle 10, his head bobbing up and down indiscriminately and his eyes going out of focus. In his bladder he had the urge to piss, but nothing came out. This had happened to him before. He stood and pushed hard, forcing the piss out of his bladder through his tubes to the base of his dick. And there it seemed to settle and hurt and build up and hurt, but still it would not come out. It was not that painful through the heroin, but uncomfortable, like the needle they stick in your pisshole when they test for gonorrhea. Zero pushed harder, but then the smack shut down his body functions even more. He put his hand against the wall to keep himself from falling backward, and splitting his head open like a piñata on the moldy vinyl floor.

Tyrone was waiting in his room upstairs. The day before,

Zero had given him some money for the heroin, but he hadn't come home until today. Zero had been disappointed, but he knew if that happened, the dope was probably good. And his standing here unable to piss was a sure sign of it. Tyrone had said to him that it would be worth the wait, and so far he had been correct in that assessment. Zero was really fucked up and knew this trouble with pissing was only one brief unpleasantry that had to be put up with. Good dope made it easier to put up with.

For the rest of the day Zero would be supremely fucked up. Zero clutched the towel bar in front of him, planted his feet firmly apart to steady himself, and pushed hard. He got a small squirt, then it all receded, it seemed, back into his bladder.

Zero could hear Ray and Henry in the sala, still drinking and screaming for the second day in a row. The television was on loud. It sounded to Zero like Soul Train, and he could picture the two of them dancing and gyrating along with the sexy and scantily clad dancers on the TV screen, like they did every weekend afternoon. The music kept getting louder. Zero could hear them screaming, "Whooooo! Whooooo! Look at that one! Look at that one!"

The H cost Zero a little bit more because he and Tyrone paid to get the connection high also. This arrangement was fine with Zero. For the past twenty years he had managed to stay out of the jailhouse through a mostly conscious effort, he liked to think. He did not want to be out on the street and have the police pick him up on charges of being a Chicano and consequently a suspected gang member, drug addict, illegal alien, parole violator, rapist, or thief. And then to have the police find the balloon of H during the routine roust would do him no good. This way it was almost like a delivery service that he paid extra for, the H being brought back by Tyrone, dressed in his security guard uniform, on the transit train.

If it was powder that Tyrone brought back, Zero would snort it up as usual. He preferred the Mexican black tar though, because of its better strength. But it was more difficult to ingest. He had to dissolve it in water first, then take it through nose drops.

Earlier, in Tyrone's room upstairs, Zero complained that it looked like someone was tapping his balloons or something, because they seemed a little light.

Tyrone was hung over and sitting on the bed with his back against the wall. He said, "It's just that those other mother-fuckers was more healthy. And let me tell you, it's still a lot better than your ass out on the streets waiting to get popped. You understand what I'm saying?"

Zero knew that Tyrone went into the balloons he got for everyone else and had no reason to believe the same was not being done to him. But, thought Zero, Tyrone was right; it was better than going out for it himself.

Tyrone rubbed his arm on the inside of his elbow where he shot up all the time and where a scar had formed long ago because of it. He scratched his lower back, then up through the middle, below the shoulder blades on both sides, then his nose. "Man, motherfucker," he said. "You know every time I go down there and try to cop for myself, these young motherfuckers, they're so stupid. They go and say that I'm the motherfuckin' po-lease.... Well, if that's the case, I oughta tell them: Hand over all your motherfuckin' dope, I'm the po-lease.... Give me a motherfuckin' break ..." His words trailed off in a yawn.

Back in the bathroom downstairs, Zero was still pushing. He could hear yelling in the sala. It sounded like insults shouted back and forth between Ray and Henry. Zero got a little spray, then held it, pushing the piss harder and harder out of his bladder. In his stomach it felt like he might vomit. The music got even louder.

When he finally finished, Zero walked into the sala and saw Henry alone with his head down on the table but with his eyes wide open and the stereo on full blast. There was a porno videotape on the TV screen. Henry sat up and fast-forwarded the picture. He stopped at a lesbian scene.

Zero stopped and watched the movie for a minute. One woman, dressed in leather chaps only, leaned forward while still standing. Another woman inserted a dildo into her pussy from behind. The movie looks good, thought Zero. The world was a happy place while he was on the H, but the loud music was too much and not good. Henry sat there oblivious to Zero and the world; occasionally he drank from a tall can of malt liquor.

Zero said, "Eh, Henry, can you turn down the music?"

Henry went on, acting as if he had not heard. He fast-forwarded through the video and stopped at a double penetration scene with one white woman sandwiched in between two black men.

In his stomach Zero had the feeling again like he needed to vomit. He was getting more and more loaded and had not yet reached the end of where the H was taking him.

Just then Tyrone walked into the sala. His lips were moving rapidly, but his voice was drowned out by the music. He walked up to the stereo and turned it off.

"Henry," Tyrone said, "you motherfucker. You gotta turn this shit down. You don't own this motherfuckin' place. You ain't the only motherfucker who lives here, motherfucker." He turned to Zero. "What the motherfuck is wrong with this motherfucker?" he asked.

"Say, bro', what's your problem?" asked Henry, menacingly. He pushed himself away from the table. His hand secretly reached across the air back behind the door where he kept a wrought iron bar broken off from an ornamental security door. It weighed several pounds, and he left it propped up in the corner for this very reason. He claimed to have the entire house booby-trapped in the same manner, with weapons all over in case he ever had some pleito, he always said.

Zero was still feeling nauseated and leaned back against the wall, out of the way and watching the dick-sucking on the television screen. One woman, down on her knees, deep-throated her male co-star. Zero moved slowly and turned toward the pair.

Tyrone went on. "Man, who the motherfuck does he think

he is? And I don't give a motherfuck!" His cigarette moved up and down violently in his mouth while he spoke. His glasses were on his face in the usual crooked manner. His eyelids looked low and heavy behind the lenses. Tyrone pushed the glasses up onto his face.

Henry stood with the iron bar hidden behind his leg. He took a short step toward Tyrone.

Tyrone was still going on. He had his hands raised above his head to emphasize his outrage. "Man, the motherfucker is gonna have to realize," he still spoke to Zero, the cigarette moving up and down in his mouth, "'cause this shit is not gonna cut it." His cigarette fell out of his mouth. "Man, motherfucking shit …"

Henry raised the iron bar in a drunken fury of blind hatred and swung it at Tyrone.

Tyrone reached down to the floor for the cigarette. Above him the iron bar crashed into the wall, digging a chunk of the plaster out of it.

Zero saw it all in slow motion, unable to do a thing about it. It looked like two cartoon characters on a cartoon show. Henry then turned toward Zero, his hand extended, still clutching the piece of iron stuck in the wall. Henry's stare was blank, void of all expression and humanity. It was the Henry no one could communicate with or control. Though they had all seen him before, no one, including Henry himself, knew this man. There was no hint of recognition of Zero in Henry's eyes. Henry might have been staring at a stranger on the Boulevard.

"I dropped my motherfuckin' ciga—" said Tyrone, startled at the crashing together of wood and metal above his head. "Motherfuck," said Tyrone. And in an instant he grabbed a tall, unopened can of malt liquor near him on the floor and with a swift motion brought the can up with all his might and smashed it square onto Henry's chin as he came to his feet.

Henry had not yet dug the weapon out of the wall when the aluminum can blew apart on impact, spraying malt liquor and Henry's blood all over the room. Henry collapsed to the floor, out cold. He lay there crumpled in a heap with his chin bleeding.

Zero stumbled along with Tyrone out the door. They left Ciudad Jimenez on a transit train, heading to Oakland. Tyrone said, "Maaaaan, I wanna get where you're at, motherfuckin' Zero." And the two of them went to look for the connection. Tyrone felt alive and would not stop talking. "Maaaaan, that motherfucker is lucky I ain't a savage. He's lucky to be alive," he kept saying over and over. He talked animatedly as the two of them strolled down West Street in Oakland.

Zero moved sluggishly, amazed he could still walk. He was flying now, and it seemed like it would never stop. And he didn't want it to.

Tyrone said, "Maaaaan, you see how I ducked. Man, I knew that motherfucker was up to something. I just had a feeling. A real tiny trace of a feeling." He sucked on a bottle of Thunderbird while they walked. Today he did not feel threatened by the police. He moved unafraid, confident he could talk both Zero's and his own way out of a ride downtown. It had been a long time since he had felt this good. And a little H would make it so much better.

"Maaaaan, I knew the motherfucker was up to something," said Tyrone. "Let me have a match?" he asked. He took the book of matches handed to him by Zero, then lit his cigarette and puffed on it rapidly. "Whooooo! Wheeeee!" he said. "That's why I went down like that. Acted like my smoke dropped out of my mouth. Shit, you know that motherfucker is lucky I didn't just kill his motherfuckin' ass. You know what I'm saying? That motherfucker is lucky to be alive." He smiled, then dug a finger up his nose.

The end of the day was bright, the sun setting over the bay before them. Zero noticed the sky above was all orange and purple mixed together.

Tyrone said, "Maaaaan, I told that motherfucker over and over and over and over and over and over and over and over and over and over and over and over and over and over and over not to fuck with me." He slurped some more wine out of the bottle.

Zero could hear the gurgling sound of the liquid as it was sucked down Tyrone's throat.

"I don't understand why the motherfucker thought he was gonna be able to chump me off like that motherfucker thought he was gonna be able to do. You understand what I'm saying? Ain't no motherfucker gonna get away with some dumb shit like that 'round me."

"I hear you," said Zero, quietly. His head was still spinning, now trying to catch up with the dope that had taken control of his body and mind. Everything around him seemed to take on a new and strangely wonderful clarity: the feel of the small warm wind against the hairs on his arms, the sidewalk underneath his feet. He scratched the top of his head with both hands as he walked, looking like a monkey while he did so. He continued scratching: his nose; then his stomach; then his sides.

Tyrone went on. "Maaaaan, that motherfucker is always talking shit like this and that, this and that, this and that, this and that, this and that, this and that, this and that, this and that, this and that, like I don't give a motherfuck what the motherfucker think or say. You know what I'm saying? But if the stupid motherfucker is gonna try and fuck me up like that, well I'm gonna have to fuck him up first.... Did you see the way I ducked on that stupid motherfucker?"

Zero tore at the side of his nose. "Man, that motherfucker is an asshole sometimes. You know that. I know that. He's lucky he's still alive. That's all I know." Zero scratched the side of his head, his face flushing red from the heroin fire inside.

"You got that right," said Tyrone. He took the bottle out of his pocket again and twisted the cap off. "Maaaaan, you know I don't like the motherfucker no how. Shit, you damn right he's lucky to be alive. But that don't mean I ain't gonna sneak down one night and slit his motherfuckin' throat." He laughed. "You see what I'm saying? Let me get another motherfuckin' cigarette?"

The pair stopped and stood on the sidewalk for a minute. Tyrone finished the last of his wine and neatly put the cap back on the bottle before throwing it in the bushes of a vacant lot. They headed toward the parking lot behind the small market on West Grand Avenue and Market Street, where Tyrone said he could find his connection. And when he found him he told him the story of what had just happened. And wasn't life good to a person, sometimes, when a man could feel so alive.

Zero was late to work on Monday morning, after sleeping for ten hours straight. Things were unusually relaxed when he walked in, and he immediately knew, before anyone had even told him, that Sarah had taken the day off.

Henry invited Zero to walk outside with him and smoke a joint in celebration. Zero could not help but wonder if Henry remembered anything. Zero himself was groggy and would remain so at least until the afternoon. On the transit train ride into Oakland Zero could barely keep his eyes open. There was no way of telling for certain when Henry was in a blackout or not. And Zero had guessed wrong before.

Today Henry looked like a mess. His cheeks looked bloated; his skin was a pale green shade and greasy, too, with a couple of large, pus-filled pimples. Zero figured Henry had slept with his face in a mess of dirt. One pimple was on the side and the other on the very tip of his nose. His chin was swollen, and he had a dirty patch of blood-caked gauze taped to the bottom of it. It looked like Tyrone had cut him good with the malt liquor can.

"I got me fucked up this weekend," said Henry as they began to walk down the street. The neighborhood was mixed: half industrial and half residential. The houses might have once been nice-looking Victorians, but not anymore. Today they were run-down and in need of paint and repairs. Truck trailers were parked up and down the street, along with wrecked and abandoned and burnt automobiles. Henry had a small, not-very-well-rolled joint to share with Zero.

"Wow, ese. Look at that!" said Zero in an exaggerated tone. "I must be seeing things, ese. I never thought I'd see you with some weed to share. It's been so long, ese."

Henry tried not to pay any attention to the comment and said nothing in response. He looked both drunk and sick: beaten and injured at the end of a long and painful road and debating what to do next. He stopped and stood for a moment in a driveway and breathed the marijuana smoke in deeply. "I been takin' care of biz, bro'," he said, squeaking the words out, while still holding his breath and the smoke down inside his lungs. He handed the joint to Zero.

"It looks like it's been taking care of you," said Zero, smiling and smoking the weed. He hoped his slight smack feeling persisted.

Henry still held the smoke in, his chest expanded, lips pursed together in his effort. He sucked the smoke in once more, for an instant, then let it out in one big cloud. "I been taking care of biz, bro'," he repeated.

"Let's keep moving," said Zero. "I saw someone looking out the window at us." He handed the joint back to Henry as they walked on.

"You and me is just alike," said Henry. "You know that, Zero? Different, but alike. Chicano, ese. You didn't never claim no barrio, but I believe you was out in those streets en

El Sur, fucked up on that sherm and juicing it. And with the pigs and the mallates, I know you know something, not everything, ese, but something 'bout what it is all 'bout." He handed the joint back over.

Zero said, "Is there anything left for me? You been holding onto that thing for so long, I thought you forgot 'bout me, ese."

Henry liked that comment, smiling. "Sorry 'bout that, bro'. I need it more today than you do."

"Crudo?" asked Zero.

"You know it, bro'," said Henry. He sang in a sing-song fashion, "Da me menudo, porque yo estoy crudo."

"I heard that," said Zero. He took short, quick tokes of the smoke. "You want the roach?" he asked.

"Yeah, bro'," said Henry. He pinched the small bit of smoking paper and pot between his thumb and forefinger and got one last toke before it was too hot to handle any longer.

They continued on, around the block. Zero lit a cigarette, even though Henry might complain. Zero wondered if Henry knew that Tyrone smoked in his room upstairs, or that Zero himself had begun sneaking them while sitting near the window in his own room and blowing the smoke outside.

Henry coughed, irritated by the cigarette smoke. "I never picked up that bad habit," he said. "I tried to, ese, but it never worked for me."

"I hear you," said Zero. "It's hard to get rid of, too."

"That's what I hear, ese."

They continued in silence for a while. Most of the activity in the area came from the factories. Zero did not know what most of them contained or what their business was. The buildings were so large and self-contained and the names of the companies so generic that no one could tell their business without asking. And Zero had never asked anyone about it before. Or thought about it either, except for today. All a person could see were the trucks picking up and delivering the boxes and pallets of whatever it was these factories did for business.

"You and me is just alike," said Henry. "You and me we're just the same way, even if you did go to college. We both learned 'bout women, sex, and love on the street corners with the homeboys, talkin' 'bout bitches all the time. So we don't know how to treat a woman right. Only how to use and abuse 'em … or anyone else, for that matter. As long as we get what we want. You know what it was like. Sabes que, ese?"

"I hear you," said Zero. "That's deep."

"I know, bro'," said Henry. "I think I got to start quitting the boozing, ese. Like you, ese. I can't be doing this no more. You know, ese? You know today I feel real funky."

"Yeah. You don't look good," said Zero.

"Yeah. I had me some pleito, ese. Chingasos. But I took care of biz. And let me tell you something, ese, confidentially. Something is going to go down, ese. You understand what I'm saying?" Henry stopped and looked over his shoulder, up and down the street. "Something is going to go down, ese," he repeated.

"That malt liquor can knock you on your ass," said Zero, smiling.

Henry stopped again and looked at Zero for a moment like he didn't quite know what Zero meant by what he said. Then Henry said, "You know it, bro'. That's what you used to drink. I still remember. You was on your WAY OUT! ese, back then. I thought they was gonna lock you up for good, ese. Sooner or later. That shit was wild." Henry looked at Zero with what may have been pride.

"That's why you and me is just alike," Henry went on. "Chicanos, somos. Que viva!" He raised a clenched brown fist in the air. "Not no gabachos. Or mallates. Pero, Chicano, ese." He stopped and did a little dance step, singing, "Que viva La Raza…. Que viva! Que viva La Raza…. Que viva! Que viva La Raza…. Que viva!" He stopped and laughed. "Boy I could use a brew," he said. "Just kidding, bro'. Ha, ha, ha. I'm gonna do better this time. Slow down.' Cause I seen how you been doing it. I been studying you, bro'. Checking you out. Ahem…." Henry cleared his throat and went on conspiratorially, "and I might got an assignment for you, ese. If you decide to accept it. C.I.A. biz, bro'. Chicano Intelligence Administration …"

"Sounds top-secret, ese," said Zero.

"Tip-top secret, bro'." Henry laughed. "Eh, I feel a whole lot better now, bro'. You ever hear from your familia, ese?"

"Sometimes," answered Zero.

"I hear you," said Henry. "You and me is just alike. You and me is the same way. My familia fucked me up too, ese. I didn't never know my old man, but I think that was better than the crazy alcoholic you had to live with, ese. I don't know how anyone can live with that shit. Or have to grow up with that shit, ese. Like my kids.... No wonder you're all fucked up, ese. When did you move away from that shit, ese?"

"When I turned eighteen," said Zero. "It was September 16th, the day I left home. Liberation day, ese."

Henry looked at Zero with a puzzled expression on his face. "Liberation day, ese?" said Henry. "What, was your familia holding you hostage all those years, ese? Or que?"

PART V

Days later Zero finally scratched off the lottery ticket. It was Friday night, and he was walking down the Boulevard, trying to keep a joint lit—some of the yesca Ray had given him. Zero liked the quiet intensity of the green leaf buzz, but it did not last long and took a whole fat joint by himself to get high.

His buzz was only halfway there when he looked up and saw a police car coming toward him. He quickly extinguished the joint with his fingertips and stuck it in his jacket pocket. "Damn," he said to himself, touching his weapon, then the lottery ticket.

He was surprised to find the ticket and took it out, thinking it might distract the police. He saw the car go by, then he heard the wheels screeching as they made a U-turn back in his direction. From out of the corner of his eye, he saw the car now at his side, moving along with him. Twice it looked like it was going to stop.

Zero held the ticket in his hand like some country bumpkin on his way to the church raffle on a Sunday night. He examined the ticket like it was the lucky one of his life, marveling at it, gawking, as the police car still went along with him. The officer riding shotgun turned toward Zero and stared at him from behind mirrored sunglasses.

Zero stopped walking and stood there for a minute scratching at the ticket, letting the squad car pass by. It kept on going, and he lingered over the removal of the silver covering on the ticket. He stood still, letting the distance increase between himself and the police as much as possible. Then he continued walking with his head down, scratching at the ticket. When he looked up the police were gone.

At that moment a carload of black teenage hoodlums honked and veered away from him as he stood in the middle of Calle 19. They jeered at him and called him names; some gave him hard stares; others threatened him. Zero ignored them and went on walking and scratching until a third and final matching amount was revealed. He looked over his shoulder, first left, then right, and continued toward home with a new spring to his step.

Outside the house on Calle 10, Zero came across Henry. He was standing in the front yard, fiddling with the garden hose and preparing to wash his car. Zero was happy and smiling and gave Henry thirty days' notice that he was moving out. Henry did not like the idea.

"You getting back together with your old lady?" asked Henry with a frown on his face.

Zero was surprised by the question. "No," he said. He had not thought of that.

"But what do you mean thirty days' notice, ese?" asked Henry.

"Yeah, Henry," said Zero. "The time has come for me to move on."

"Well, whatever, ese," said Henry. "But you know we agreed on sixty days' notice."

"What do you mean?" asked Zero.

"We agreed on sixty days' notice, ese. In cased you ever wanted to move out."

"I don't think so," said Zero, more surprised than irritated.

"You know, ese," said Henry. He turned away and began playing with the nozzle on the hose. He spoke over his shoulder. "The way I remember it is that we agreed on two months notice before moving out. Tha's 'cause I don't got no deposit from you on the room. And in cased you ever tried to fuck me over."

Zero turned his eyes toward the sky in exasperation.

"That's what I remember, ese," said Henry. He turned and saw Zero.

"Henry, this is bullshit."

"That's the way I remember it," said Henry, trying not to look angry.

A silence fell over the two of them. Off in the distance a dog could be heard barking. A car driving by honked at them, but neither of them responded.

Finally, Zero said, "Eh, you know it sounds like maybe I'm the one getting fucked."

"Eh, ese, I don't think so," said Henry.

"Yeah, I know you don't," said Zero. He walked on into the house.

In the hallway Zero ran into Pancho. It was the first time in weeks the men had seen each other. They walked to the back of the house.

"Eh, who opened my door?" asked Zero.

Pancho was drunk and dazed. His breath smelled like crap. "I don't know, ese," said Pancho. He swayed on his feet. "My door was open too when I got home. You better check your stuff out. I didn't see nothing gone in my room."

Zero looked around. All he saw was the regular mess of clothes scattered over the shelves and bed and chair and dresser, along with books, magazines, and newspapers. "It looks okay to me," he said.

Pancho hung in the doorway still. He had a can of beer with him now. "Everything okay?" he asked.

"As far as I can tell," said Zero. He casually peeked into the closet for a second and saw the boxes filled with his belongings stacked up as they were normally. He waited for Pancho to leave before checking his hiding place.

Later Zero went upstairs to see Tyrone. The two of them stood outside on the top landing of the stairs, looking out over the backyard. Tyrone smoked a cigarette and took swigs from a bottle of Thunderbird.

"Let me have a cigarette?" asked Zero.

"It's menthol," warned Tyrone.

"That's okay." Zero took the cigarette and found some matches in his back pocket.

Tyrone drank long and hard; his throat made gurgling sounds when he swallowed. "Whew!" he gasped, coming up for air. He then began to flap his arms and step bowlegged in a circle for a few seconds, cackling like a cartoon chicken. He shouted, "Thunderchicken!" then stood still again and dragged on his cigarette.

"So you say you wanna see the man," said Tyrone. "How much money you got?"

Smoke curled out of Zero's nostrils. "Yeah. I got my vacation pay already."

"Say, check that out," said Tyrone. He pointed down into the yard.

Alexander was standing in the yard talking to a tall, thin man wearing narrow-legged black jeans, big black boots, and a yellow t-shirt. The two men stood close together, their faces right near each other's. Alexander put a hand on the other man's belly.

"Shit, let's get away from these white motherfuckers," said Tyrone. With a flick of his fingers he tossed his cigarette butt down near the pair. It sailed over their unsuspecting heads. "Let me get my coat," he said, "and we'll go down and see the man." He slipped the wine bottle into his pants pocket. "How much money you got?"

"I got a hundred-dollar bill," said Zero. "I'll get you high too."

Tyrone caught his breath. "A hundred dollars? Damn, let's go. And you damn right you getting me high too, motherfucker. Damn, what did you do, hit the numbers, or what?" The pair stepped into the upstairs hallway.

"I'm moving out too," said Zero.

Tyrone stopped walking. "Damn, you really did hit the numbers, I guess. I know you won't forget your buddy Tyrone now. Getting back together with your old lady?"

"No," said Zero, unsure. "I'm just getting my own place."

As they walked along they could hear the stereo down below blasting out loud funk rhythms. Tyrone stopped outside his room. "You let motherfucker Henry know you moving out?" he asked.

The two stepped into the room.

"He didn't like it," said Zero.

"Fuck that motherfucker," said Tyrone. "He don't got to like it. Too bad you can't stick aroun' for me killing that motherfucker. He don't know it, but he's living on borrowed time." Tyrone took the bottle out of his pocket and finished off the wine.

"He started saying some crap about sixty days' notice," said Zero.

"Right," said Tyrone. He put the empty bottle on top of his television. "That motherfucker tries that shit with everybody, I hear." He grabbed a green camouflage army jacket from a hook behind the door. "I hope that motherfucker got some good shit today," he said. "Let's go."

The big Low N' Slow carshow was coming to the Civic Plaza near the end of the month. Everyone was talking about it— even Tyrone planned on attending. Joe heard about it and called Zero from the Central Valley, hundreds of miles away. Zero told only him the details of his good fortune.

Joe said, "Yeah, Zero, I'll drive up there. I heard it's gonna be big. Real big. I heard Thee Midniters are gonna get back together to do a show, all the way from East L.A."

Zero said, "I didn't hear about that."

"Yeah," said Joe, "and WAR too. That's what I heard."

"Wow," said Zero. "I didn't hear that either."

"It's gonna be live," said Joe. "I'll drive up. I got some weed."

Zero could hear Joe striking a match, then begin taking long noisy drags on a joint.

"Yeah, I know," said Zero. "That sounds good."

An incessant banging started at the front door.

"Eh, hold on a minute," Zero said to Joe. He put the phone down on the table and went into la entrada. He called out, "Who is it?"

There was more banging on the door. In the background Zero could hear Ray's voice.

"Eh, it's me," said Ray. "Open up, cabron."

Zero opened the door. Ray and Henry stood there obviously drunk. Henry carried in one hand the new and improved sixty-four-ounce jug of malt liquor. Zero suspected the brown grocery bag that Ray carried was filled with more jugs. Ray clinked when he moved.

"What's happening?" asked Zero.

Ray answered, "Orale, Zero, how you doing?"

Henry said nothing, trying to look both innocent of the banging on the door and aloof, with a glazed look in his eyes.

"Forget your keys?" asked Zero.

Henry only smirked, saying nothing.

Ray said, "Yeah, you know how it is, ese."

"I'm on the phone," said Zero.

"Sorry, man. Sorry," said Ray. "We'll be quiet. We'll be

quiet." He put a fingertip to his lips. "Shhhh …," he said to Henry as they both walked inside.

Zero headed back to the sala.

On the telephone, he said, "Eh, Joe, that was just Ray and Henry."

"Payasos?" asked Joe.

"Yeah, you know it," said Zero. "Hold on again." He covered the telephone mouthpiece with his hand and held it down at his side.

Ray and Henry walked into the room. Henry stomped his feet and banged into the walls. Ray followed him with a big grin on his face, struggling to hold in his laughter. The pair proceeded through the sala and on into the kitchen. Ray clinked as he passed by.

Zero pulled the phone as far as he could over to the other side of the room and looked over his shoulder. He had a partial view of Henry leaning against the sink in the kitchen and drinking from the jug. Ray stood in the doorway, his back to Zero. Henry leaned in toward Ray, appearing to whisper.

Zero spoke low into the telephone. "Eh, Joe," he said, "I wanna hear what they're saying. Okay? Just hold on."

"I'll go get something to drink," said Joe. "I'll get on the line when I get back."

"Go ahead," said Zero. He stood there with the receiver still to his ear. He turned slightly, glancing through the doorway, and could see Henry smiling and drinking. Henry's smile faded when he saw Zero. Zero turned back away.

Henry and Ray began laughing, then talking loudly.

Ray said to Henry, "So tell me again what you would do if someone fucked with you?"

"Yes, well, I would be forced to fuck them up," said Henry. "Fuck them up for fucking with me, ese."

Zero looked into a mirror on the wall right there in front of his face. In the reflection he could see the back of Ray's head as he tilted it to take a drink from the jug. Ray put the empty bottle down near his feet, then stood back up.

"Give me another cerveza, Henry, homeboy."

Zero turned slightly again and saw Henry move across the doorway from east to west. There was the sound of the refrigerator opening, bottles hitting each other, then the door closing. Henry moved across the doorway from west to east.

Ray said, "You're crazy, homeboy, Henry. I thought someone was gonna call the pigs on you las' night, shooting your cuete like that into the sky."

"Nobody fucks with me," said Henry. "I'll go psycho-loco on a motherfucker who tries to fuck with me. You know what I mean, ese?"

Ray said, "Hey, what kind of cuete was that anyways? It looked like a fuckin' cannon. That shit was baaaad. You almost blew my ear drums out, ese."

"You like that motherfucker, huh?" said Henry.

In the reflection Zero saw Henry grin and take a drink from the jug of malt liquor.

"Don't drink it all, motherfucker," said Ray. "I still want some. Hijole, look at that backwash, motherfucker."

Zero saw Henry still held the jug up, his forefinger hooked

into the handle on the neck. He tilted the jug back for another drink.

"Cabron," said Ray.

Henry finished drinking, then wiped the jug opening with his palm before handing it to Ray.

"Cabron," said Ray. "Don't wipe that with those hands. I know you don't never wash them."

"That's just extra flavoring," said Henry.

"Cabron," said Ray, now holding the jug in both of his hands. He tilted his head to drink.

Joe came back on the telephone line. "Eh, Zero," he said, "what's going on?"

"Just bullshit," said Zero. "Where'd you go?"

"To get something to drink," said Joe. "Eh, you know they got these new sixty-four-ounce jugs of malt liquor now?"

"Yeah, I know," said Zero. "I've seen them."

"You tried it yet?" asked Joe.

"No, I haven't drank in quite some time."

"You're missing out."

"Yeah, I know."

"They still in the other room?"

Zero looked in the reflection. "Yeah, they're still there," he said. "I better get going.... So you're coming up for the car show?"

"Fuck yes," said Joe. "People from all over this great lowrider nation are gonna be there, Zero. And Chicanas, ese, looking fine like a bottle of wine. I wish she was mine, ese."

"Yeah, sounds good," said Zero. He lowered his voice even

more. "When you get here," he said, "I'll have the money from the state. We're gonna get us some good stuff."

"I hate to say this," said Joe, "but they ain't gonna pay you nothing for a couple of months at least, ese."

"You're kidding," said Zero. "What do you mean?"

"No, I'm not," said Joe. "It takes that long for the pinche state to process the claim. Eh, you know it's a great big beautiful bureaucracy that I work for."

"Yeah, I guess," said Zero. He thought about all the money he had been spending lately, expecting his big cash prize to be in his hands before he had to move.

"Are you sure?" asked Zero.

"Yeah, I'm sure," said Joe. "But don't sound so down. Look, I know somebody who'll buy the ticket from you, cash money, but he's gonna give you less, you know. He'll probably give you half of what it's really worth, but cash. And a lot sooner than the state will. That's for sure."

"You think so?" asked Zero. "About this guy?"

"Yeah, I'm sure," said Joe. "He does it all the time. I'll call him and set it up. You'll have to come down here probably. Maybe you want to stay a few days?"

"Yeah, that sounds good," said Zero. "My vacation starts a couple of days before the car show. I'm off that whole week, but I'm supposed to move in the middle of it."

Zero did some quick arithmetic in his head. If he only got half of what the ticket was worth, he would still have more money than he ever had in his life. Company Printing gave him nearly three hundred dollars for his vacation pay. And he had just over two hundred saved up. It would all add up to almost three thousand when he got the prize money. I could try something new, he thought. Some place new. I could live in the Valley for a while and tell La Wilma I need to do something else for a while. But that I still love her and plan on marrying her someday when my head is on straight about my own life, let alone a life together with her.

"How long can I stay?" asked Zero.

Ray and Henry started up again with their noise making. Zero looked into the mirror.

Ray said, "Man, you're gonna see me at the Low N' Slow car show, ese, and I'm gonna be fucked up, ese. No lie."

"Simon, ese," said Henry.

Ray went on. "There's gonna be lowriders from all over the place, ese. And Chicanas, ese, looking fine like a bottle of wine. I wish she was mine." He drank from the jug of malt liquor.

Joe asked, "What's going on?"

"Just talking shit," said Zero.

Henry shouted from the other room. "Eh, I hope my ex-bitch don't show up, ese. But I'm gonna be cool 'bout it."

Zero whispered into the phone. "How long can I stay?"

"As long as you want," said Joe.

"Your old lady won't mind?"

"She split," said Joe. "I mean, I threw her out.... It'll be like old times back in college. I'm going out with this fine young thing now."

"Before or after your old lady left?" asked Zero. "Just kidding. Okay, then it sounds like you got a deal. You talk to your man and let me know what's happening when you come up for the show."

"Orale, carnal," said Joe. "I better go now. See you."

"Yeah, see you," said Zero. He hung up the phone.

One Thursday night Zero went to tell La Wilma. He met her after work, and they walked down to the nearby Chinese hole-in-the-wall restaurant for a quiet dinner. They ordered their usual: chicken fried rice, shrimp chow mein, and pot stickers. Zero always went overboard with the hot oil. And the waiter looked at him strangely because he insisted on eating with chopsticks. Zero poured hot tea for both of them. La Wilma opened the fortune cookies.

Afterward, instead of waiting for the bus, they walked back to her place. The night was warm and clear with a strong breeze blowing in from off the bay. The trees all around were full and green. They enjoyed each other's hands in their own as they strolled past the crowded cafés, bookstores, restaurants, and antique shops on College Avenue.

Zero thought La Wilma was looking especially good that night. "Did you lose some weight? Or what?" he asked. There seemed something different about her since the last time they had seen each other, but he couldn't figure it out.

"Why do you say that, ese," said La Wilma. Her big mouth opened in a smile that included her eyes.

"You look good is all," said Zero. La india, he thought, with your long, straight black hair and dark, smooth complexion. He thought her features were both hard-edged and elegant at the same time: the sharply angled nose, prominent cheek bones, and eyes that slightly slanted.

Later they lounged about on the carpet in the living room of her apartment. The lights were all out inside, and the lamppost in the courtyard outside the window cast its shadow on the wall. They laughed and talked for a while before stripping naked when it got dark.

La Wilma put on a fishnet body stocking that Zero had given her. Her big brown nipples stuck out through the holes in the mesh. They made love aggressively, La Wilma on all fours and Zero behind her. On the record player Sunny and the Sunglows beckoned *Talk to Me*.

During the night Zero awoke with La Wilma's mouth on him. He swelled up inside it. Then they rolled themselves out of the covers. La Wilma turned away from Zero and squatted over him. He ran his hands lightly over her back and ass while she wiggled her pelvis back and forth, then up and down with just the knob of him disappearing in and out of her with a juicy squish sound. She sat down on his full length, squeezing her muscles inside, then again her pelvis went back and forth, next up and down a few times. She then rode the length back up and started all over again.

In the morning Zero waited down on the corner for the bus to take him to work. It was already late in coming, just as he had been afraid it might be. The sun was bright and bared down on him. He had a jacket on but did not want to take it off because of the wind. He looked around for some shade, but there was none nearby. The heat became unbearable, so he took his jacket off. The hairs rose up on his arms.

Zero scratched the side of his nose a bit, then noticed the taste in his mouth. What is it? he wondered. He scratched the side of his nose again. Dirt. Metallica. The good mother earth. He touched his tongue to the roof of his mouth, and there it was. Morfina. He scratched the back of his neck and for a second felt a little light-headed. There was an itch in his throat like he wanted to throw up.

Zero backed up to the car dealership on the corner and leaned his back against the building. It was all glass on the first floor, the showroom. He slid down the glass, squatting in the sunshine. He closed his eyes; his head was swirling. Blue, red, and green sparkles played on the insides of his eyelids.

Someone shouted, "Hey you!"

Zero opened his eyes; his vision was all blurry. He turned toward the voice.

"Get away from the building before I call a cop," said the voice.

When his vision cleared up Zero saw a red-faced white man standing, not far away, in the doorway of the dealership. He was wide-shouldered and dressed in a blue suit and red tie. His blond hair was short and parted on the right side. He looked like a former high school football star, now with a beer belly and bushy moustache.

Zero was startled and struggled to his feet. The sparkles began to blur his vision again.

The man said, "Stay away from the building, amigo. Or I'll call el police-oh." He walked back into the building.

Zero stumbled over to the curb. He felt cold and put his jacket back on. The cars were speeding by, east and west, in front of him on MacArthur Boulevard. He leaned against the metal bus stop pole, then touched his tongue to the roof of his mouth. Dirt. Metallica. There it was. The good mother earth. He slid down the pole until he was squatting with his back against it. He lowered his head and closed his eyes. Red, blue, and green sparkles played on the insides of his eyelids. Morfina. He started to sweat in the bright but clammy sunshine.

On the day of the big Low N' Slow car show the sun was blazing down onto the lawn of the Civic Plaza. Salsa rhythms floated out over the heads of the dancing throng near the stage in front of City Hall. The trees along the perimeter were all draped in green, white, and red tissue paper. Earlier in the day there had been contests: a dance contest, a bikini contest, a Mr. Muscle contest, and, for the cars customized with hydraulic lifts, a car-hopping contest.

The lowriders had come from all over: Fresno, East L.A., La Frontera, Stockton, Sacramento, and San Pancho. Every other minute a grito could be heard coming from one of the mostly Chicano men, women, and children assembled. On the outskirts of the crowd was a large group of policemen on horseback and on foot, looking for the first opportunity to go into the crowd and break it all up. But today north and south, and everywhere in between, were gathered together in peace.

Zero sat with La Wilma and Joe. Joe had brought along his new girlfriend, Rosario. She was a young Chicana from East Los Angeles who was in her first year in college. Earlier in the day Joe had told Zero about her.

"Big breasts, big eyes, big hair, and the right attitude," Joe had said. "And she's mature for her age, too." Joe had then winked.

The four of them sat in the middle of the more than one thousand people.

Zero rubbed the side of his nose, stood, and looked out over the crowd. He thought he saw Tyrone on the other side of the lawn, leaning his back against a tree and nodding out. It looked like Alexander sat next to him. Alexander had red hair and wore tortoiseshell glasses. He handed a bottle of wine to Tyrone.

Down at the very front of all the people Zero saw Henry and Ray. The both of them were screaming and howling, standing in the sun and sweating, bare-chested and burned all over. Henry took a drink from a bottle of beer. He wore a broken sombrero and the bottom half of his running suit. The back of his pants looked stained. Henry turned toward the back of the crowd and howled, "Oooooooooowwwwwwwwww!" He had a big smile on his bloated face and began to dance with Ray. Ray looked like a lunatic. He wore cut-off jeans and dark glasses with a bandana tied tightly around his head, gangster fashion: low on his forehead, almost covering his eyes. His rolls of flab flapped in the wind and sunshine as he moved his big body as best he could to a rhythm no one else in the crowd seemed to hear. The pair danced with each other and then with some young cholas standing behind them. Henry drooled openly over the girls' teenage bodies.

The band stopped playing, and the crowd up front sat down. Only Ray and Henry stayed on their feet.

Zero, his pants legs pushed up, scratched his shins with both hands moving at the same time. His hair felt like it was on fire. He reached up and scratched it. His face felt flushed. He went back to his shins. They were beginning to bleed. He pushed the pants legs down and sat on his hands.

It was the itchy and scratchy period. Sometimes he could not help but scratch himself bloody, waiting for the nod. But today he knew the nod would probably not come from the codiena. Leroy had given him some Number 3s on his last day before vacation. Zero was never going back to that job. Codiena has no kick, he thought.

La Wilma turned toward Zero. "Eh, ese, what's happening with you?" she asked.

Zero felt like he was in a goofy narcotic fuzz and did not answer. His hands looked swollen. He tried to hide them by sitting on them, but he needed one of them to rub the side of his nose.

"What's wrong with your hands, ese?" La Wilma asked sternly.

Zero mumbled, "I'm telling you that Tylenol shit is dangerous."

"What, ese?" La Wilma glared at him.

Joe and Rosario turned toward Zero also. Joe looked down at Zero's hands, then up to his face. He stared at him for a full minute, then took a swig of his beer. Rosario was wide-eyed. She looked liked she had never seen such a thing before.

"Are you okay?" asked Rosario. She sounded worried.

Zero tried to smile. He could not figure out what Joe's look had meant. His face and brain felt on fire. His fingers were swelling up fast.

Joe said matter of factly, "Eh, you better take that ring off your finger."

The sweat dripping from Zero's face caused streaks of dirt down the sides. "Fuckin' asshole, Leroy," muttered Zero. His words felt thick in his mouth.

"What are you on?" asked La Wilma. She seemed to be going to a great deal of trouble to control her anger.

"Just some weed and codeina," said Zero, trying to pass it all off as just some silly joke gone awry. "No big deal. I'll be all right."

"Fuck you," said La Wilma. She turned away from Zero, looking toward the stage.

"You better take your ring off," said Joe, now embarrassed for his friend.

Zero smiled weakly and pulled on the ring on his right hand. It wouldn't come off. "Damn," he said to himself, then he began twisting the ring back and forth, trying to get it over the swollen knuckle. Then he rubbed the side of his head.

La Wilma turned toward him. "You think I'm stupid, ese?" she asked.

Zero was feeling more groggy. "No, I didn't say that," he said.

"Fuck you, Zero," said La Wilma. She turned back away.

"How's it going?" asked Joe, trying to act like everything was normal.

La Wilma's eyes darted over toward Joe.

Zero answered Joe. "Okay, I guess," he said. He started on the finger again, moving the ring back and forth, trying to twist it off. He tried pulling on the ring with his other hand, but stopped to rub his head. He pulled again on the ring, and it seemed like it began to slip.

"Eh, I think I got it," said Zero, casually, as if nothing was the matter, as if he didn't know that La Wilma was obviously very angry with him, as if it were perfectly normal for a grown man to go out to a car show with some friends, eat a handful of pills, and then later find his hands beginning to swell up while his head was in a hazy narcotic fuzz buzz. He turned toward the stage, trying to act like he was interested in what was going on up there. He tried to hide his hands. Then he would need them to scratch his arms and the side of his head.

La Wilma turned and stared at him.

He was lost in his own little world, scratching his head, then arms and nose. He pushed his pants legs up again and started on his shins. He went back to his arms and began to draw blood. There were others in the crowd around him who also began to stare.

Zero started on his ring again. He twisted it back and forth. "Eh, I think I got it," he said, twisting, then pulling, twisting, then pulling. It finally came off, and he rolled over backwards in his effort. "I got it covered," he said, sitting back up. He ran his fingers through his hair, then began scratching his head, trying to get at the fire he felt burning out of control just beneath his scalp.

La Wilma stood and said to Joe, "I'll see you." She gathered her purse and sandals, slipping them on her feet. "Nice to meet you," she said to Rosario. She turned and glared at Zero, not saying anything.

Joe said, "Hey, don't go, La Wilma. Everything's gonna be all right. Come on, enjoy the show. Have a cerveza."

La Wilma did not sit back down. "I'll see you," she said, ignoring Zero and walking alone through the crowd toward the Boulevard.

The last night at Calle 10 Zero had to do his laundry. He had woken up at 10 PM, still groggy from the last dose of Demerol, and after having slept for the last twenty hours. The room was dark and nearly empty, but his ghetto blaster was still there. It was one of the few items he did not get rid of. He turned on the all-news radio station to find out what day it was. Then he gathered up all his clothes and took them to the 24-hour laundromat.

It was just after 1 AM when he came back. The #72 pulled into the parking lot of the transit station. Zero got off with a few other passengers. The box he carried was big and awkward. He held it out in front of him and had to stretch both his arms around it to keep a hold of it. The clothes were stacked high, and he kept his chin down on top of them to keep them from falling. From his right hand dangled a plastic grocery bag. Inside were six cans of Hot and Spicy V-8. They were for the journey to the Valley in the morning.

Zero moved off the bus sluggishly. He continued on through the dark and quiet parking lot. The few others that had got off also disappeared into the night. Zero struggled with the box of clothes. On the bus he had been having a hard time staying awake. The cans of V-8 swung at his side.

Near some bushes a tall black man emerged from out of the shadows. "You got a cigarette?" he asked Zero.

"No, I don't have anything," Zero lied. It would have been too much trouble for him to find one right now, and he wanted to hurry home and get off the streets. As he walked away Zero thought that maybe the man's face was familiar. Then he remembered seeing him before out in front of the Liquor Locker begging, tweeking, twitching, and schizting for a blast of crack. Once he had even seen him getting arrested for stealing from the Liquor Locker.

Zero hurried up. While he walked he tried to control and savor the fuzzy feeling that was still all over him. He went across the Boulevard.

On the other side the same crackhead appeared from the side of a building. "You got a cigarette," he said. This time he was immediately in Zero's face.

"No," said Zero. He stopped just in time, stepped back some, then to his left and around the man.

The crackhead grabbed onto Zero's jacket sleeve. The cans of V-8 swung heavily back and forth. Zero had his head down on top of the clothes pile. He tried swinging his body away to wrest the jacket free from the crackhead. It did not work.

"You have money," said the crackhead. His eyes were all bugged out. Saliva flew from his mouth. His lips looked severely chapped.

"Eh, fuckhead." Zero's speech was garbled. He struggled to get free and not knock over the clean clothes.

"Yeah. You got any money?"

The crackhead pulled down on the jacket sleeve, steering Zero. The two moved forward in a tango, heading out into the middle of the street.

"Let me have your money. I got a gun, motherfucker."

The crackhead pulled down on the sleeve with one hand; the other reached back to his own jacket pocket furthest from Zero and stayed inside there.

"I'm gonna shoot you, motherfucker. Give me your money."

Zero struggled with the box in front of him. The V-8s swung back and forth. "Get the fuck away from me," said Zero, pulling in the opposite direction. The cans of tomato and chili drink slapped his thighs. He pressed his chin down harder onto the piles of clean clothes.

"I got a gun, motherfucker. Give me your money."

The crackhead pulled down on the jacket sleeve, pulling Zero forward. The pair went out into the street with their tug-of-war, the crackhead doing the steering and Zero caught in the momentum of it all.

"Get the fuck away from me," said Zero, pulling back, his chin still on top of the clothes, the cans swinging. The sleeve was pulled forward, the jacket slipping off more and more, beginning to come up his back.

"Give me your money, motherfucker. I got a gun."

The crackhead stepped backward, pulling down on the sleeve. He kept his other hand hidden in his jacket pocket.

"I got a gun!"

The crackhead kept his hand in his jacket pocket.

"I got a gun!"

"Get the fuck away from me!"

The handles to the plastic grocery bag strained, then snapped. The cans crashed to the street. Zero's jacket slipped off over his head.

The crackhead moved now more deftly backward, pulling the sleeve down farther.

"I got a gun!"

The jacket went over Zero's head.

"Get the fuck away from me!"

The box fell out of Zero's hands. He followed it down, falling hard on both his knees.

"I got a gun!"

The crackhead skirted away from Zero. He stood a few yards away, not knowing what to do next.

Zero struggled to his feet. He threw the jacket off entirely.

"Hey, fucker!"

"I got a gun, you crazy motherfucker."

The crackhead moved further away.

"Stupid motherfucker!"

Zero had his hands balled into fists. He was up on his feet and started toward the crackhead.

The crackhead took off running.

Zero followed him back to the Boulevard then stopped.

The crackhead continued.

Zero watched him head back across the transit station parking lot, through the bushes, over a fence, and then down near the train tracks. He walked back to his clothes. They were all over the street. He bent down and began piling them into the box.

a little help para los amigos gabachos

cabron	asshole
calcos	shoes
Calle 10	Tenth Street
carnal	brother
chi-chis	breasts
chingasos	fighting, throwing blows
cholas	female Chicano gang youth
ciudad	city
Ciudad de las Calles	City of Streets
coloradas	reds, barbituates, downers
crudo	hung over
cuete	gun
El Club Paraiso	The Paradise Club
ese	you, hey you
gabachos	Anglo-Americans
hijole	damn
mallate	black man
moscos	flies
nariz	nose
orale	hey, it's okay
pachucos	Chicano street youth of '30s and '40s
perro callejero	a dog in the street
pinche	damned
pleito	trouble, fight
polvo	Angel Dust
San Pancho	San Francisco
simon	yes
vato	guy, dude
yesca	marijuana